A FIELD GUIDE TO MERMAIDS

A
FIELD
GUIDE TO
MERMAIDS

EMILY B. MARTIN

HENRY HOLT AND COMPANY
NEW YORK

To the water protectors, scientists, and conservationists
And to my mermaids, Lucy and Amelia

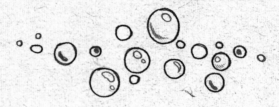

Henry Holt and Company, *Publishers since 1866*
Henry Holt® is a registered trademark of Macmillan Publishing Group, LLC
120 Broadway, New York, NY 10271 • mackids.com

Our books may be purchased in bulk for promotional, educational, or business use. Please contact your local bookseller or the Macmillan Corporate and Premium Sales Department at (800) 221-7945 ext. 5442 or by email at MacmillanSpecialMarkets@macmillan.com.

Library of Congress Cataloging-in-Publication Data is available.

First edition, 2022
Book design by Aurora Parlagreco
Printed in China by RR Donnelley Asia Printing Solutions Ltd., Dongguan City, Guangdong Province

ISBN 978-1-250-79432-1 (POB)
1 3 5 7 9 10 8 6 4 2

CONTENTS

INTRODUCTION

A glimmer of fish scales.

A splash from a colorful fin.

The echo of a mysterious song across the water.

Few mythical creatures are more instantly recognizable and yet more mysterious than mermaids. Whether seen perched on a rock at the water's edge or spied only as a dim outline beneath the waves, mermaids have long fascinated sailors, scientists, storytellers, and surprised onlookers alike.

But how can one spot a mermaid? What are the clues that mermaids might live in a certain body of water? How do mermaids in one kind of habitat differ from others? Do mermaids only exist in huge expanses of open water, or could there be mermaids in the tiny creek or pond near you? This book aims to help you examine aquatic habitats with a careful eye to find signs of mermaid activity and think about what kinds of mermaids they might be.

HOW TO USE THIS GUIDE

Mermaids exist in all kinds of water and have many different adaptations to survive in their particular environment. This guide breaks down these habitat types into sections and discusses the characteristics of the mermaids in each one. Questions at the beginning of each section will get you started in your exploration of the illustrations on each page, as well as the real aquatic habitats you find in nature.

WHAT IS A MERMAID?

A mermaid is a living being that has the torso, arms, and head of a human and the tail and fins of a fish or, in some cases, a marine mammal such as a whale or manatee. Most can breathe both above and below water, while some are permanently aquatic and never venture above the surface. Those that spend time out of the water must remain damp to survive, which they accomplish through a variety of adaptations and learned behaviors. Mermaids are among the most powerful swimmers in any aquatic habitat, and they can even crawl over land for short distances to seek out new bodies of water. While there are some that are tolerant of pollution, most mermaids require clean water to survive.

Caudal Fin

Gills

Webbing

Dorsal Fins

Pelvic Fins

Scales

HOW DO MERMAIDS BREATHE?

Mermaids are born with external gills that let them absorb oxygen from the water. Then they go through a metamorphosis when the gills disappear, and they develop lungs. These allow them to breathe above water, but unlike marine mammals, they don't have to surface for air. Instead, they absorb oxygen from the water through their skin, like a newt.

Mermaids are capable of their own speech and are thought by most scientists to be as intelligent as humans, though they are generally wary of people. Their songs are known to be incredibly complex. Many mermaids have built amazing homes, villages, and even cities underwater that rival any architecture on land.

Mermaids aren't only female. The collective term is *merfolk*, but in this book we will be using the word *mermaid* throughout. No matter their gender, merfolk usually mimic the patterns and coloring of native fish in their habitats, and they all tend to share a similar love for eye-catching jewelry.

THE MERMAID LIFE CYCLE

Mermaids give birth to live young, just like whales and dolphins. These babies are called *naiads* and begin life completely aquatic, with webbed hands and frilly external gills. Despite these amphibian-like characteristics, they nurse from their mothers like mammals and spend most of their time snuggled against their mothers or learning to swim.

As naiads age, their hands become less webbed and their gills disappear. Their lungs develop, which means they can begin making their first trips to the surface.

Gills

MERMAID SPECIES

Mermaids can be classified in one of two ways. Because mermaid adaptations are so tied to their homes, one of the easiest ways to categorize mermaids is by habitat. This is a handy way to identify mermaids that may have different colors or patterns and yet share the same range. For example, a mermaid mimicking a sauger and one mimicking a smallmouth bass, both found in the Ohio River, could each be referred to as a river mermaid.

To get more specific, mermaids can also be referred to by the type of aquatic animal they mimic, such as referring to a tuna mermaid or a dolphin mermaid. Mimicking the colors, patterns, and adaptations of other animals in their habitats assists with camouflage, obtaining food, scaring away predators, and communicating with other mermaids. An easy way to identify mermaids in your area is to look up your native fish, amphibians, and aquatic mammals and determine what animals a local mermaid might mimic!

> *Most of the mermaid species in this book are depicted with the animal they mimic in the same illustration.*

MERMAID DIET

Mermaids eat a variety of things depending on their habitat. Most are omnivorous, eating both plants and meat, though some tend to eat more of one or the other. A mermaid in a forested swamp, for example, would have plenty of vegetable life to choose from, while a mermaid in an icy sea would rely more on fish and other creatures.

MERMAID HABITATS

In general, mermaids can live in any water source a fish can. They can be found in salt water, fresh water, and brackish water, and they are adapted to a wide variety of environments, from muddy swamps to the open ocean. Some prefer deep water, where they almost never see the surface, while others are happy in water so shallow it merely keeps them damp. However, in almost all cases, mermaids require clean water. They don't tolerate pollution well and have been known to abandon streams or coastal areas with high levels of toxins or debris.

In some instances, mermaids have been known to leave a water source and scoot or crawl to another one. This puts them at risk for drying out—plus it's hard work! Nevertheless, some mermaids have been found in isolated pools or lakes they could only have crawled to. Possibly the most famous example is the Pacific Tarn mermaid, who was discovered in the highest named lake in the country, at over thirteen thousand feet in the Colorado Rockies!

HABITATS IN THIS GUIDE

Moving Fresh Water

These are habitats like streams and rivers, full of changes and energy.

Still Fresh Water

These include lakes and ponds and tend to be stable, reliable habitats.

Wetlands

These habitats have fluctuating amounts of water and can be salty, fresh, or brackish—a combination of both.

Coastal Water

These saltwater environments fringe land and are home to some of the most busy and diverse mermaid ecosystems.

Open Ocean

This is the biggest habitat type, but one of the least populated, split up by the amount of sunlight available.

Extreme and Unlikely

Whether harsh, remote, or just surprising, these are environments where you might not expect to find mermaids!

PRACTICE MERMAID SAFETY!

Always be safe when you are exploring water habitats! While searching for mermaids is fun, remember that water can be dangerous if you're not careful. Follow these guidelines and other water-safety rules, and always tell someone where you are going.

Keep Yourself Safe

Know the rules of the place you're in—if you're in a protected park, some areas may be off-limits, or certain activities like rock or shell collecting might not be allowed.

Do not climb or jump on wet rocks, especially around moving water. Falling on slippery rocks is one of the main ways people injure themselves around water.

If you are in a boat or playing around deep water, *always* wear a life jacket, even if you know how to swim.

Keep Mermaids Safe

If you pick up a rock to look under it, be sure to put it gently back exactly where it was—creatures may depend on it for shelter.

Avoid changing the habitat you're in, including building rock dams and digging out banks.

Never litter, and if possible, gather trash you might see. But always do this with gloves and a trash bag, and don't try to reach trash that's too far away or too big.

Practice water conservation at home—turn off taps when you don't need them, take shorter showers, and don't leave hoses running.

Check with your city government, or at your local community centers and parks, to see if there are programs where you can learn more about protecting water ecosystems near you!

MOVING
FRESHWATER
MERMAIDS

LIFE IN MOTION

Tiny springs bubbling up in high mountain meadows, thundering cascades churning with white foam, broad channels winding lazily toward the sea—life in streams and rivers is one of constant motion and change. Everything from food to rocks to trash tumbles down with the current. Floods scour the riverbed, changing the pattern of the banks. Water leaps over hillsides and boulders to form rapids and waterfalls. The mermaids who live in moving water are energetic and adaptable—just like their environment.

The smallest bodies of moving water are springs and brooks, which gather into streams and then into rivers. The nature of the habitat within them depends largely on what kind of land they're passing through—rocky banks create rapids, while sandy banks create a gentler current. Some mermaids prefer the shallow, gravelly sections known as riffles, while others prefer the deeper, calmer pools, and yet others like the currents found in open channels.

When you are exploring streams and rivers to look for mermaids, you can ask yourself these questions:

- Do I know where this water comes from and where it flows to?
- Is the water shallow or deep? Is it clear or cloudy? How might that affect mermaids?
- Is the bottom rocky or sandy? How does that affect the movement of the water?
- Are there any obstacles mermaids might encounter?
- How might activities that happen upstream affect mermaids downstream?
- If I were a mermaid, what might I like about this habitat? What might be a problem?

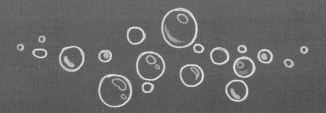

Spotted
Salamander

Red-Cheeked
Salamander

Red Eft

Hellbender

Stonefly

HEADWATER STREAM MERMAIDS
Little River, TN

Up in mountain highlands, clear, cold springs bubble out of the ground and rush over rocky beds, between mossy banks, and under shady canopies. These are the birthplaces of great riverways, and they're prime habitats for small creatures that like their water cool, swift, and clean.

Mermaids in headwaters tend to be small and highly suited to life in these tumbling streams. They are strong swimmers, able to fight against turbulent currents and leap small cascades with little trouble. These mermaids are highly protective of the small, sensitive species sharing their homes. In the Little River in the mountains of Tennessee, for example, mermaids have a special relationship with *endemic* salamanders, and can often be found cuddling at least one of the amphibians as a

ENDEMIC: *native to one specific location and nowhere else in the world.*

HIGHLAND RIVER MERMAIDS

Arkansas River, CO

Tiny mountain streams run together to form fast, rocky highland rivers. At these elevations, the water is pure, cold, and full of oxygen, like the headwaters of the Arkansas River in Colorado. These highland ecosystems can be both ideal and challenging for mermaids—while the water is less polluted than farther downriver, seasons bring intense change: ice and snowbanks in the winter, and foaming floods from snowmelt in the spring.

Mermaids in the Mountain West have a special relationship with American dippers, the United States' only aquatic songbird. These pudgy little birds can dive into the water and walk along the bottom, feeding on aquatic insects. Mermaids often trail along with them, turning over rocks to reveal insect larvae.

American Dipper

Cutthroat Trout

Blue Catfish

Higgins Eye
Pearlymussel

Purple Wartyback
Mussel

Winged
Mapleleaf
Mussel

FLATLAND RIVER MERMAIDS

Mississippi River, WI, IA, IL, MO

As they leave the mountains, highland rivers merge and become wider, slower, and sandier. One such river is the powerful Mississippi, which collects water from over half of the states in the US.

Flatland river mermaids are some of the largest and longest-living mermaids. Many of them have a passion for a very humble creature: the freshwater mussel. For a long time, scientists assumed this was because of mermaids' fondness for pearls, which are created by mussels in fresh water and oysters in salt water. But there's another reason for mermaids to care so much about these little shell creatures—mussels are vital to a healthy river ecosystem. They filter out nutrients and pollution, storing both in their bodies. Mermaids can often be seen lovingly tending their shell gardens in an effort to keep their rivers clean.

COASTAL RIVER MERMAIDS

Elwha River, WA

As rivers reach the coast, some become warm and slow, spreading out into swamps and marshes, while others are cold and fast, like the Elwha, which rushes out of the mountains to meet the sea. These rivers are home to *anadromous* mermaids—mermaids who spend most of their lives in the ocean before traveling into coastal freshwater rivers, along with many kinds of fish. The fish make this journey to lay their eggs; likewise, mermaids make this journey to have their babies in the same safe, protected streams they were born in.

The swim up these coastal rivers is never easy—mermaids have to fight against rapids and leap up cascades, dodging predators all the while. Some swim for miles to reach their safe, familiar childhood streams.

Sockeye
Salmon

MERMAID TAILS

One of the most eye-catching and important features of any mermaid is her tail. These tails can come in all shapes, sizes, and colors, and they can mimic the tails of almost any kind of aquatic animal. Many mermaid tails are covered in scales, which help protect their skin and decrease drag through the water. Other tails are covered in smooth or rough skin, bony plates, or even waterproof fur, like a seal!

Most mermaids also sport fins on their tails. These are membranes that help them maneuver and balance in the water. Fins can be spiny, fleshy, or soft and flexible like fabric. Usually, fins come in pairs, with one pair on either side of the mermaid below her hips and another pair along her spine. The fin at the end of a mermaid's tail is called a *caudal fin* and can come in a wide variety of shapes. Mermaids with forked or heterocercal tails are the fastest swimmers—they're often found in ocean environments, where there's lots of room to build up speed.

CAUDAL FIN SHAPES

Forked

Lunate

Truncate

Rounded

Pointed

Heterocercal

Another important feature of a mermaid's tail is the *lateral line*. This is a sensory organ that runs down both sides of a mermaid's body that helps her detect movement and electrical charges in the water. This means that even in very dark or murky water, mermaids can sense the approach of objects and other animals, which helps them navigate their environments without relying on their eyesight.

Lateral Line

The depth of water affects how different mermaids move—those in shallow water, like streams, tend to move their tails side to side, while those in deep water, like the open ocean, often move their tails up and down.

BRAIDED RIVER MERMAIDS
Platte River, NE

Just like the strands of braided hair, braided rivers are made up of many meandering water channels that part and weave. These types of rivers carry sand and silt from upriver and deposit them as midstream islands that shift all the time. These wide, shallow waterways and the constantly changing islands within them create havens for all kinds of animals, especially migrating birds.

Mermaids in braided rivers navigate the winding waterways with ease. They can often be spotted lounging on the sandy islands, safe in the middle of the river. When threatened, they will slip back into the water and dart into the maze of interwoven river channels, becoming almost impossible to find again. They play a role in protecting important stopover grounds for migrating birds, like rustling up the minnows, frogs, and insects for them to eat, and chasing away predators.

18

Pallid Sturgeon

Whooping
Crane

Sandhill
Crane

CREATURE FEATURE

Whooping Cranes—Named for the "whooping" sound they make, these are the tallest birds in North America.

Sandhill Cranes—These birds are highly social and can flock together in the thousands.

BLACKWATER RIVER MERMAIDS
Suwanee River, GA, FL

Don't be alarmed by the dark color of the water—it's perfectly natural and a highly unique ecosystem. Blackwater rivers are usually found flowing through swamps, like the Suwanee River, which begins in Okefenokee Swamp in Georgia. The water is darkened by chemicals called *tannins* seeping out of decaying plants, turning it the color of tea. Though the water might look dirty, these tannins actually help purify it.

The current tends to be slow, and because of all the decaying life in the water, these rivers are low in dissolved oxygen. This means blackwater river mermaids are often found lounging partially out of the water, sunning on logs or banks with other animals and taking deep breaths of humid air with their lungs.

Sparkling Jewelwing Damselfly

Yellow-Bellied Sliders

Redbreast Sunfish

Bowfin

Yellow Perch

FREEZING RIVER MERMAIDS

Sheyenne River, ND

We're used to thinking about mermaids and other aquatic creatures in summer. But mermaids don't have the option to climb out when it gets too cold—they live in water all year round. So what do they do in the winter?

As temperatures drop, river mermaids face unstable conditions, with ice that forms, freezes, and breaks apart in unpredictable, sometimes dangerous ways. Ice first starts to form in tiny crystals that pile up, creating slush called *frazil ice*. This mushy ice can shift unpredictably, making it difficult to find a safe place to stay. Frazil ice can sometimes freeze in patches below the surface, creating *anchor ice*. This can build up into dams, draining pools downstream and cutting off mermaids and other animals from safer habitats.

But mermaids aren't helpless. Some simply migrate downriver to warmer waters, or even to the ocean, to wait out the winter. Others are builders, constructing shelters to protect themselves and their vulnerable underwater friends during the cold months.

Mountain
Laurel

Eastern
Blackbanded
Darter

Turquoise
Darter

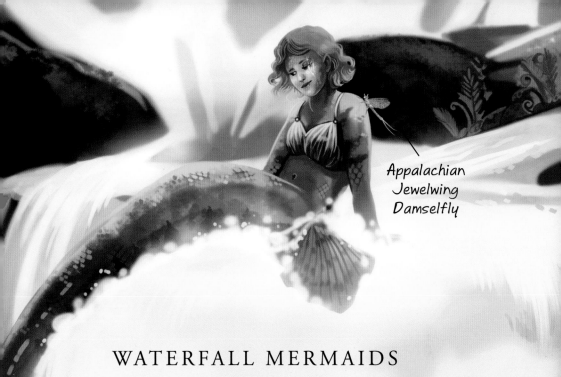

Appalachian
Jewelwing
Damselfly

WATERFALL MERMAIDS
Big Bend Falls, SC, GA

Where the land drops away, waterfalls abound. Plunging downward, these falls can take the forms of wide curtains, dramatic ribbons, churning flumes, rippling cascades, or murmuring trickles. No matter their appearance, all waterfalls have significant impacts on the surrounding environment. They churn up oxygen and nutrients, hollow out pools, and create lush habitat along riverbanks that mermaids love.

Exceptionally tall or powerful waterfalls are natural barriers, though some strong mermaids will always manage to climb rocky slopes to reach the higher waters. Gentler waterfalls serve as favorite meeting places for upstream and downstream relatives.

CREATURE FEATURE

Darters—These small, quick fish are some of the most colorful freshwater fish in the United States. They only live in clean moving water and are often found only in a few small ranges separated by abundant waterfalls.

CANYON RIVER MERMAIDS
Colorado River, AZ

Moving water is a powerful force—whether as a trickle or a flood, it can carve its way through solid rock, leaving behind cliffs, mesas, and canyons. Many of our most dramatic landforms were carved by flowing water, and few rivers have created more stunning scenery than the Colorado River. On its way down from the Rocky Mountains, it has cut a path for itself through the arid Southwest, forming some of our most well-known and best-loved landmarks, like the Grand Canyon.

Life for a mermaid in a canyon river like the Colorado can be full of surprises. Canyon mermaids must be on their guard for heavy rapids, sudden rises or drops in water levels, and boulders careening downstream. They are experts at navigating the cloudy, churning waters and thrive in the sun-warmed shallows and deep secret pools.

Humpback Chub

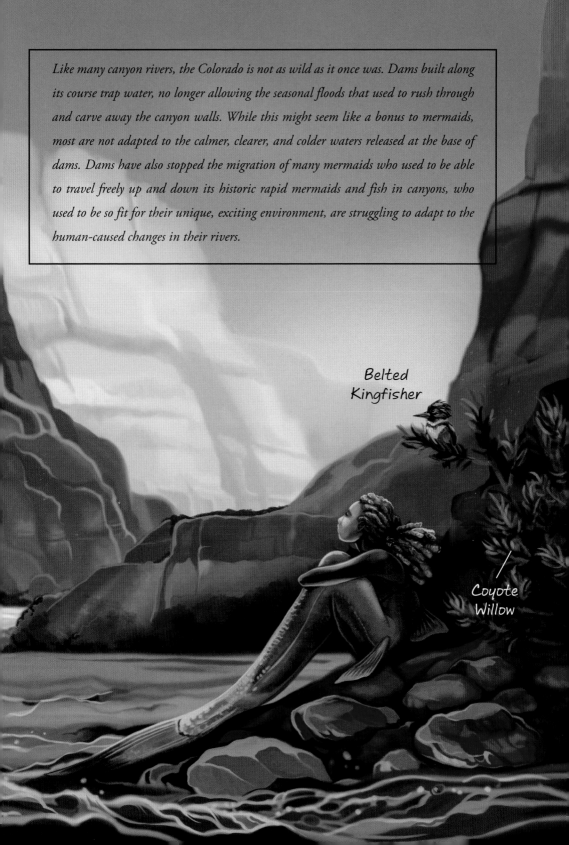

Like many canyon rivers, the Colorado is not as wild as it once was. Dams built along its course trap water, no longer allowing the seasonal floods that used to rush through and carve away the canyon walls. While this might seem like a bonus to mermaids, most are not adapted to the calmer, clearer, and colder waters released at the base of dams. Dams have also stopped the migration of many mermaids who used to be able to travel freely up and down its historic rapid mermaids and fish in canyons, who used to be so fit for their unique, exciting environment, are struggling to adapt to the human-caused changes in their rivers.

Belted
Kingfisher

Coyote
Willow

KARST SPRING MERMAIDS
Jacob's Well, TX

Karst is a type of landscape that forms when water wears away the rock around it, especially limestone. This erosion forms caves, sinkholes, and underground rivers. Sometimes these rivers bubble up to the surface, forming karst springs that flow into lakes or streams, such as Jacob's Well in Texas, which flows up into Cypress Creek.

Unlike rivers that are completely hidden in caves, water in a karst spring may disappear into the ground in one place and emerge in another after traveling through the underground maze of dissolved limestone. This means that despite the appearance of living in a small creek, mermaids in these types of karst habitats can actually travel incredible distances through flooded tunnels and underground rivers. Agile and canny, they can slither through sometimes small openings in the rock that connect one underground passage to another.

Bluebonnet

Guadalupe
Bass

Zebra
Mussels

Round
Goby

Sea Lamprey

Eurasian
Watermilfoil

CANAL MERMAIDS
Erie Canal, NY

Canals are human-made rivers. In the days before highways and airplanes, canals were the best way to move heavy cargo around, and many are still used today for shipping.

Canals also changed the environment, connecting bodies of water that had never been connected before. When the Erie Canal was completed in the 1800s, mermaids from the Atlantic and the Hudson River could now make their way into the Great Lakes, and vice versa. And while this gave some opportunity for making new friends, it also let in a host of *invasive species*, like sea lamprey, which preyed on lake trout, and aquatic weeds, which crowded out native plants. Even new mermaids put strains on the ecosystem. These days, mermaids use canals to travel and visit new places, but they also patrol them to keep down invasive plants and animals.

INVASIVE SPECIES: *a plant or animal not native to an ecosystem that causes damage to native species. The plants and animals shown here are invasive.*

URBAN RIVER MERMAIDS
Delaware River, NJ, DE, PA

Big cities often spring up along rivers—after all, the more people in one place, the more water they'll need to drink and use for cooking, cleaning, and working. Rivers have also played a vital role in travel and shipping, whether in small canoes or giant barges. All this activity means that urban rivers are busy, crowded places. In many cases, it also means they are polluted and blocked by human-made objects like dams. For a long time—and still in some ways today—rivers were used as dumping grounds for sewage, garbage, and other waste; eventually, many species have been driven out, unable to survive.

American Eel

Mermaids, like so many other aquatic animals, need clean water and the ability to travel freely through their habitat. This is why mermaids are often absent from urban rivers. But some cities have worked to restore the health of their water. The Delaware River, which provides drinking water to many major cities on the mid-Atlantic coast—like New York City, Philadelphia, and Trenton—is now the longest river in the United States that doesn't have a dam on its main stem, which means mermaids and fish can travel the same routes they always have. This provides an important habitat for *catadromous* mermaids and fish, which are the opposite of *anadromous* mermaids and fish (see Coastal Rivers for more). Catadromous fish, like the American eel, migrate from fresh water to spawn in the ocean. Thanks to the undammed water and lower pollution of the Delaware, catadromous mermaids are still able to swim out to sea to have their babies.

Striped
Bass

29

STILL FRESHWATER
MERMAIDS

WIDE-OPEN WATER MERMAIDS

Of all the water on earth, less than 3 percent of it is fresh water, and most of that is frozen in glaciers and ice sheets. But of the little bit of unfrozen fresh water that's left, most of it is found in lakes—and what an amazing variety of lakes there are! Whether scooped out by retreating glaciers, broken open by earthquakes, or gradually formed by flowing water, lakes are bodies of fresh water, usually deep enough to have changes in light and temperature. A pond tends to be a body of water too small and shallow to have much difference in temperature from top to bottom.

Mermaids in ponds and lakes prefer all kinds of different habitats. Some like the thick plant life around the edges, or *littoral* zone, while others like the open water near the middle of the lake, or the *limnetic* zone. Some like the warm, sunny surface water, and some like the deep, darker water near the bottom. Some happily venture into the rivers spilling into and out of a lake. Some remain their whole lives in the still water.

No matter where they live, lake mermaids are playful, curious, and occasionally, mischievous—all over the world are tales of strange sightings of bizarre creatures in lakes. If these sightings aren't mermaids themselves, they're often some kind of construction they've made to bewilder humans on the shore.

When you are exploring ponds and lakes to look for mermaids, you can ask yourself these questions:

- How deep is this water? Might the temperature and light be different at the bottom than the top?
- Are there plants in the water? How might mermaids use them?
- Is the water clear or murky? Warm or cool?
- Are there places on the shore a mermaid might like? Are there buildings or structures that have changed the shoreline?
- If I were a mermaid, what might I like about this habitat? What might be a problem?

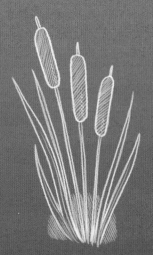

POND MERMAIDS

A farm pond, KS

When studying mermaids, it's tempting to focus on the famous, flashy ones living in coral reefs or powerful rivers. But mermaids can be found in even the humblest aquatic habitats, even tiny farm ponds. Typically small and well camouflaged, these mermaids are nevertheless some of the most common and easily spotted species in the United States.

> INDICATOR SPECIES: *a plant or animal whose presence or behavior gives important clues about the conditions of their environment.*

A quiet life in shallow water means pond mermaids are highly attuned to the environment around them. They're some of the only mermaids who pay attention to the stars, and they can predict upcoming weather with surprising accuracy based on the temperature, moisture in the air, and shape of the clouds. These shallow-water mermaids can also be important *indicators* of water quality and habitat health.

Spotted Bass

Beaver

BEAVER POND MERMAIDS

Deep Fork, OK

Many ponds and wetlands are specially built—but not by humans. Beavers are experts at building natural dams, which cause water to build up behind them. These ponds spread out water to the surrounding floodplain, creating important wetlands and preventing erosion downstream.

Many mermaids in small backwater environments depend on beaver ponds as reliable havens. When drought occurs or temperatures rise, beaver ponds preserve a stable, cool habitat where mermaids and fish can shelter. During hard winter freezes, mermaids may seek out beaver ponds to escape shifting ice in rivers. Because of this, mermaids have been known to help build and repair beaver dams, and some have even been seen slapping the water with their hands, mimicking the

GLACIAL LAKE MERMAIDS
Lake Superior, MI, WI, MN

If you traveled back in time over ten thousand years ago, the United States would have looked very different. Giant ice sheets covered much of the continent, and as they moved slowly over the earth, they shaped the ground underneath, carving out valleys that would later fill in with water to become lakes. Many lakes in the United States were carved by these massive, ancient glaciers, including our biggest lake—indeed, the biggest freshwater lake in the world by surface area—Lake Superior.

Because Lake Superior is so big, it supports a huge array of mermaids. While all these mermaids have their own special roles in the ecosystem, one major task they all participate in each year is what's known as "turning over" the lake. Most lakes are divided into layers based on temperature—in the summer, warm water floats near the surface, while colder water stays at the bottom, separated by the thermocline, or the boundary between the two. But in winter, these layers swap, thanks to the surface waters cooling down and becoming more dense. This means that twice a year, the water mixes, and the usually separate layers all swirl together. These turnovers are times of great celebration for mermaids—many of the largest, most exciting mermaid festivities occur as lake mermaids get together and help churn the lake. This work distributes nutrients and oxygen evenly through the water, ensuring a healthy habitat for all the other plants and animals that live there.

Lake
Sturgeon

CREATURE FEATURE

Lake Sturgeon—These are some of the largest freshwater fish in North America, reaching up to eight feet long! They can also live to be over 150 years old—that means some lake sturgeon alive today could have been born before the invention of the modern automobile!

FAULT-BLOCK LAKE MERMAIDS

Lake Tahoe, CA, NV

The earth's crust is constantly moving in big plates that form a shell around the planet. These plates grind and slip against each other, making the ground buckle, break, sink, and rise. This action is called *tectonics*, and the places where the plates touch are called *faults*. All this movement creates giant landforms, sometimes rising up to become mountains or sinking to form valleys. When water from streams or rainfall fills tectonic valleys, they become fault-block lakes, and they're some of the oldest and deepest lakes in the world.

Mermaids in these deep fault-block lakes often stick to particular zones in the open water, just like mermaids in the open ocean. Some prefer the warm, sunny waters near the surface, while others like the cold, dark depths near the bottom—in a place like Lake Tahoe, on the border of California and Nevada, that can be over a thousand feet deep! The steep sides and plunging depths of these lakes provide lots of room for mermaids who like the freedom of open water, compared to their cousins in shallower lakes who prefer weedy environments.

Lahontan
Redside

American
Bullfrog

Broadleaf
Arrowhead

Channel
Catfish

OXBOW LAKE MERMAIDS

Lake Chicot, AR

As a river twists its way across the plains, sometimes it decides it wants to take a shortcut. When a river erodes away a new path, it can leave behind an oxbow lake—a curve of the river that has become dammed with sediment on either end, creating still water in the shape of a big *C*. Often these lakes are surrounded by swamps and bogs—in fact, the country's largest oxbow lake, Lake Chicot, in Arkansas, which used to be a meander of the Mississippi River, draws its water from nearby bayous. Oxbows are a great example of how water is constantly changing the landscape around it, always looking for the quickest way downhill.

Mermaids in oxbows tend to be shy and secretive. They like hiding in lots of weedy growth. In a natural habitat, mermaids like to stick to these weeds and roots, but lacking that, they will also shelter under boat docks. Some people even install human-made shelters under the water for fish and mermaids—mermaids will often supplement these by cultivating their favorite plants and mussels around

MERMAID COLORATION AND PATTERNS

The diversity of mermaid appearances is endless, from riots of vibrant colors to perfectly camouflaged neutrals. However, these colors and patterns aren't accidental—they all serve a purpose. Whether they're a warning sign to predators, an attractant to other animals, or a clever disguise, a mermaid's unique colors help her survive, hide, and, yes, show off in her environment.

One common feature shared by most mermaids is *countershading*—meaning they have darker colors along their backs and paler colors along their bellies. This is an easy method of camouflage for many aquatic animals. Think about it—when you look down into the water, things are often shadowed and murky. But if you're underwater and you look up, the sky creates a light-colored background. If a mermaid was all darkly colored, she would show up easily to predators swimming underneath her, while if she was all lightly colored, she would be easily visible from above.

Mermaids can have all kinds of patterns—stripes, spots, blotches, vertical bars, and saddles. These patterns are like human fingerprints—no two mermaids are exactly alike. Like some species of butterflies and moths, they can also have eye-spots on their tails to startle predators. Their fins and tails can also be shaped or patterned like elements of their environments, such as seaweed, coral, or pebbles, to help them avoid detection.

Some mermaids have the ability to change color, like a chameleon, to adapt to their surroundings. They might change color depending on the depth of the water or time of day, or their colors and patterns may shift as they age. Some merely change colors to blend in with their environment, and some change colors depending on what they eat. For example, a mermaid who eats mostly shrimp may appear pink.

CRATER LAKE MERMAIDS
Crater Lake, OR

Crater Lake, in Oregon, was formed in a huge volcanic eruption over seven thousand years ago. The bowl it left behind, called a *caldera*, filled with rain and snow and has become the deepest lake in the United States.

Mermaids thrive in the clear, clean water in crater lakes—if they can reach them. The mermaids that have migrated to a remote, rugged place like Oregon's Crater Lake must have made an arduous climb to reach the pristine water. Mermaids could have also been accidentally introduced to the lake in the same way nonnative fish were. In the late 1880s, baby fish were carried in buckets from nearby rivers and dumped into the lake so people could go fishing. Could mermaid naiads also have been caught in those buckets?

Rainbow Trout

Mazama Newt

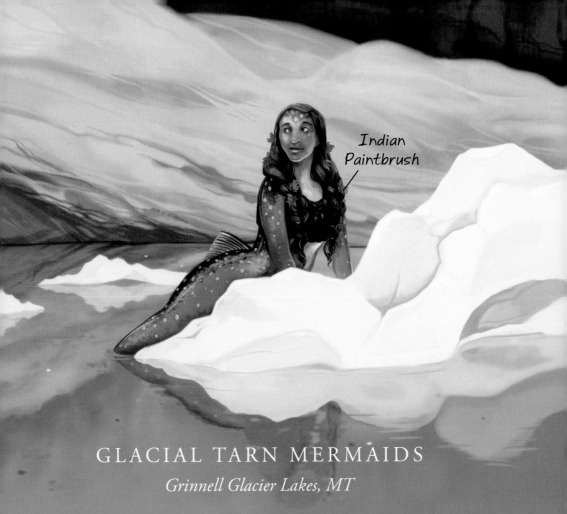

GLACIAL TARN MERMAIDS
Grinnell Glacier Lakes, MT

Tarns are formed when a glacier scoops out a bowl in the earth and then fills it with water as the glacier recedes. Tarns at the feet of still-active glaciers, like Grinnell Glacier in Montana, often have icebergs floating in them during warm months, broken off by the glacier's slow retreat. They also contain glacial flour, or powdered rock ground off by ice, which can turn the water milky white or turquoise.

Because tarns are found high up in rocky mountain valleys near active glaciers, only the hardiest and most intrepid mermaids can inhabit these lakes. They frequently have to make their way up frigid streams studded with rapids and waterfalls, and winters are long and extreme. Not many other animals join them—these waters are just too harsh and low in nutrients.

TROPHIC LAKE MERMAIDS
Lake Michigan, MI, WI, IL, IN

One major factor to survival in lakes is the amount of nutrients in the water. Lakes with low nutrients are very clear and clean, with lots of dissolved oxygen. As nutrient levels go up, more and more plants and algae start to thrive. And while plants are the basis of most food webs, there can be too much of a good thing. As plants and algae decay, they use up oxygen, which robs it from the water. Too much growth, and suddenly there's not enough oxygen in the water for mermaids and other animals. Those that can flee the water might do so; those that can't have to rely on breathing above the surface.

Lake
Whitefish

Midge
Larvae

Leeches

Gizzard
Shad

This process of rising nutrients in water is called *eutrophication*, and it happens naturally to many water sources, both fresh and salt water. But human activity can make eutrophication worse, as chemicals from farms, fertilizers from lawns, or waste from sewers runs into streams and lakes. In Lake Michigan, for example, the water in most of the lake is clear, clean, and well oxygenated, making excellent habitat for mermaids. But in one urban area, Green Bay, the runoff from the city has turned the water murky, smelly, and full of algae. Mermaids who make their homes in Green Bay frequently head out to visit their relatives in the "country" of the cleaner waters to take a break from the cloudy water in the bay.

RESERVOIR MERMAIDS
Kentucky Lake and Dam, KY

A lake made by humans, whether dug or dammed, is called a reservoir. These artificial lakes are usually made to store drinking water, irrigate crops, control flooding, provide hydroelectric power, and create places for people to go boating, fishing, and swimming.

Dams can be tricky for mermaids. They interrupt the natural migration paths of river mermaids, and those in reservoirs often have to deal with sediment building up in the water and fluctuating levels of nutrients and oxygen. But many mermaids make do. They tend to be shy, as they often are in human-built spaces. They make an effort to shoo fish and other animals away from the dam itself, which can be dangerous if they get too close to the big turbines and spillways that let the water out on the other side.

Bluegill

Emerald
Shiners

Mink

FREEZING LAKE MERMAIDS

Lake Vermilion, MN

Few wintertime sights are as beautiful as a frozen lake carpeted with sparkling snow, spreading out between the icy trees. But can anything survive below the ice? Yes! The layer of ice on top insulates everything beneath it, creating a stable, safe habitat for the creatures below.

Some mermaids and fish prefer to spend the winter at the very bottom of the lake, where the water is warmest. Their bodies slow down, and they enter a state almost like hibernation. Other mermaids are more active in the cooler upper layers throughout the winter. The main danger for lake mermaids in the winter is running low on dissolved oxygen—the ice above keeps the air out, and if winter lasts too long, the animals below can run short. Sometimes mermaids will take it upon themselves to keep holes in the ice open, or enlist the help of otters or mink to do it for them.

WETLAND MERMAIDS

THE WIDE WORLD OF WETLANDS

Swamps, marshes, bogs . . . these places might be considered unpleasant, even useless, by humans, but they're some of the most unusual, vibrant, and important ecosystems on the planet. They filter water, recycle nutrients, control flooding, and provide protected habitats for baby fish and thousands of other animals. Healthy rivers and coasts wouldn't exist without healthy wetlands.

And besides all that, they are *prime* places to find mermaids!

So what is a wetland? It's pretty simple to define a lake or river, but venture into the world of wetlands and things can become as murky and mysterious as the habitats themselves. A wetland is an environment that is flooded with water—sometimes for only part of the year, sometimes permanently. There are many different kinds of wetlands—the main way to tell the difference between them is what kinds of plants grow there. You'll see trees in a swamp, grasses in a marsh, and mosses in a bog.

Within these three main categories, wetlands can be saltwater, freshwater, or brackish water. They can be seasonal or year-round, and they frequently run into each other and mingle, creating pockets of different habitats within a great, soggy, interconnected ecosystem.

Different plants, salt levels, and flood patterns mean different kinds of mermaids. Wetland mermaids are some of the most diverse in the world, as well as the most adaptable, able to tolerate huge fluctuations in their environments. Wetland mermaids also tend to move overland more than any other species, often when changing water levels leave some areas cut off from main channels. The damp nature of wetlands helps keep them from drying out as they crawl to new water.

When you are exploring wetlands to look for mermaids, you can ask yourself these questions:
- Where does the water here come from, and where does it go?
- Is there water here all year long, or just sometimes?
- What are good hiding places for mermaids?
- If a mermaid had to find new water, where might she travel to get there?
- If I were a mermaid, what might I like about this habitat? What might be a problem?

FRESHWATER MARSH MERMAIDS
Camas Creek, ID

Freshwater marshes are the most common type of wetland in the United States, and appear in all different varieties—vast, soggy meadows surrounding lakes; small basins in fields or forests that fill with water; wet flats along rivers; and even holes left behind by melting glaciers. The main thing that separates marshes from other types of wetlands is that they're mostly filled with water-loving grasses like bulrush and cattail.

Mermaids prefer marshes that have a reliable water source that won't dry up completely when the summer comes. But even so, marsh mermaids can survive and thrive in surprisingly little water—sometimes all they need is a few inches over mud, and they can dart around with amazing agility. Fish in marshes tend to be limited to permanent ponds and creeks, but the wet grasses are perfect for all sorts of birds. Mermaids are often found protecting nests hidden in the rushes, and helping hatchlings learn to swim.

Trumpeter Swan

Marsh Rabbit

Cordgrass

ters

Fiddler Crab

SALT MARSH MERMAIDS
Cumberland Island, GA

Visit a salt marsh in the morning and then come back in the afternoon, and you might think you had visited two different places. Like many coastal habitats, the water in salt marshes is constantly rising and falling with the tide. At high tide, they look like mazes of flooded grasses and open waterways; at low tide, mud or sand flats are exposed, threaded with tidal creeks, and busy invertebrates like fiddler crabs are visible scuttling across the dark mud. This mud is deep, squishy, and smelly—all signs that it's rich with nutrients that fuel these busy ecosystems!

Mermaids are frequently visitors in salt marshes, swimming among the cordgrass at high tide and heading back out to sea as it retreats. But when they feel safe enough, they may stay after the tide goes out, lounging on the mudflats and carefully selecting empty shells for jewelry. Salt marshes are plentiful places to find beautiful and unusual shells, and many mermaids will travel long distances to reach the same favorite collecting spots.

MERMAID JEWELRY

Mermaids are renowned far and wide for their elaborate and whimsical accessories. Crowns, necklaces, earrings, bracelets, rings—no ornamentation is too gaudy or too complex. Free from the stronger effects of gravity, mermaids are able to create elaborate jewelry from almost any material they find in their habitat.

Pearls

These glinting, iridescent gems, adored by mermaids for their beauty, are formed by some saltwater oysters and freshwater mussels. These animals are types of *bivalves*, which consist of the animal's simple body protected inside a hinged shell. If an irritating bit of sand or debris makes its way into the shell, the bivalve coats it with layers of shiny mother-of-pearl, eventually building it up into a pearl. This mother-of-pearl also coats the insides of the hinged shells, which make the shells themselves much sought-after prizes for jewelry.

Shells

Other shells are prized for their beautiful shapes, striking colors, or delicate patterns. Shells are exterior skeletons for a huge variety of invertebrate animals, including snails, clams, and scallops. Mermaids also love turtle shells and even eggshells. Mermaids are careful not to harm the creatures relying on these shells for protection, preferring to collect them after they've been discarded.

Living Creatures

Both pearls and shells are created by living creatures, but there are some organisms that mermaids will put to work as accessories while they're still alive. Anemones, sea sponges, sand dollars, urchins, and starfish can all be coaxed into adorning a mermaid's crown or hair, and they're generally amenable enough to be used for decoration. Occasionally, this is even a mutually beneficial relationship, with the invertebrate snacking on whatever else the mermaid has added to her jewelry.

Other sources of mermaid jewelry include seaweed, wildflowers, insect wings and cases, shark teeth, and coral.

Decorator Crab

CREATURE FEATURE

Decorator Crab—These crabs pick up bits of seaweed, rocks, or even living animals like anemones and urchins and attach them to their shells as camouflage!

FRESHWATER SWAMP MERMAIDS
Great Dismal Swamp, VA

Sweeping tree trunks soar straight from the water. Branches curl down to skim the surface, trailing moss. Noisy life bursts above, below, and all around. Welcome to the swamp! Here the main plants are trees, particularly ones that like wet feet, like the loblolly pine and bald cypress.

Swamps are excellent habitats for mermaids, thanks to the wide variety of food sources and shelters. These are some of the most vocal mermaids—the swamp is a noisy place, day or night, full of the calls of birds, frogs, mammals, and insects. The mermaids here are no different, joining in with their own songs that echo among the trunks. Swamp mermaids are unusual in another way—some of them climb trees! On humid days, they can sometimes be seen draped over branches hanging over the water. When they are startled, be prepared for a mighty splash as they leap into the water and swim away.

Bald Cypress

Northern
Pearly-Eye

Snapping
Turtle

Switchcane

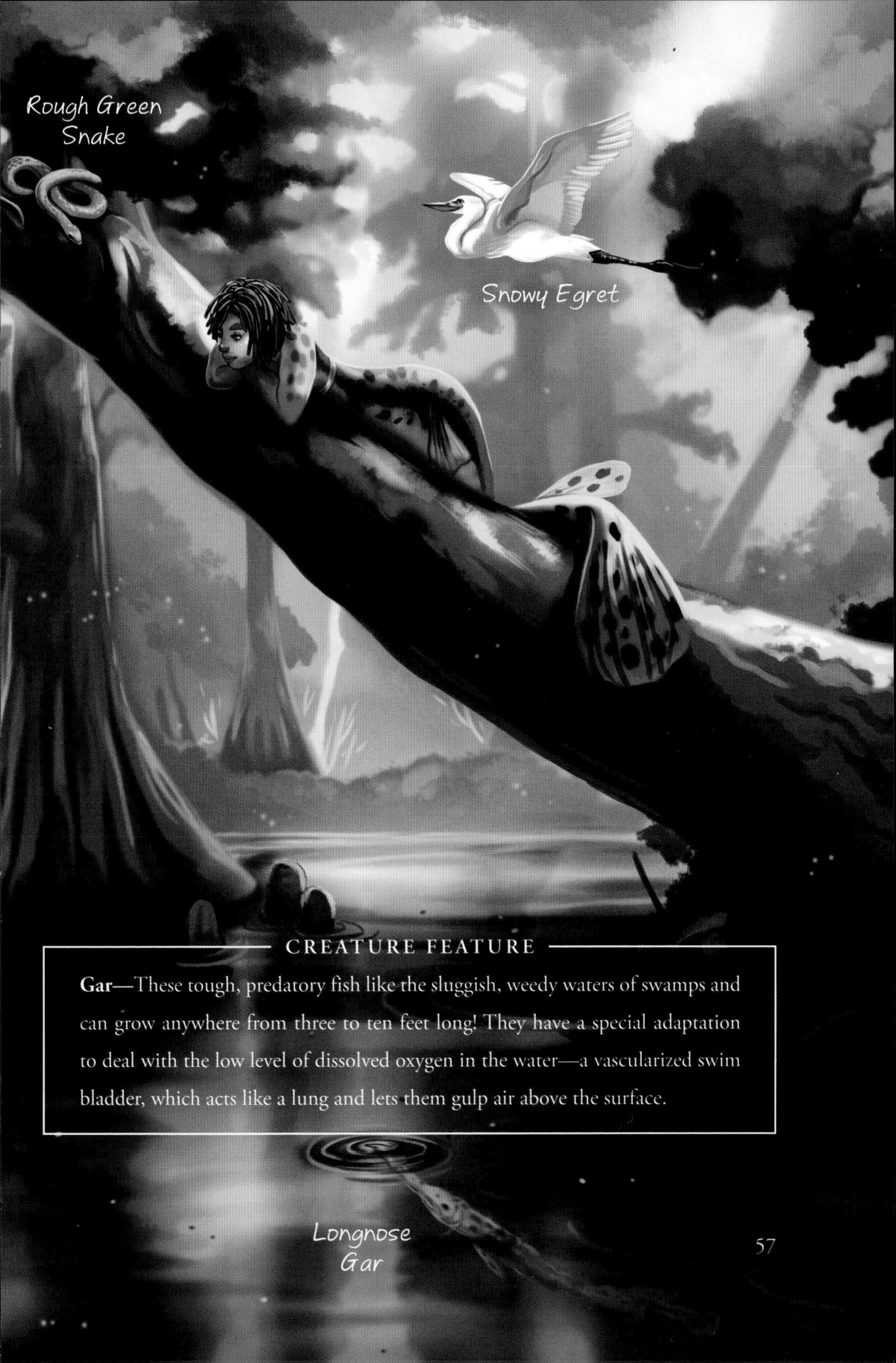

Rough Green
Snake

Snowy Egret

CREATURE FEATURE

Gar—These tough, predatory fish like the sluggish, weedy waters of swamps and can grow anywhere from three to ten feet long! They have a special adaptation to deal with the low level of dissolved oxygen in the water—a vascularized swim bladder, which acts like a lung and lets them gulp air above the surface.

Longnose
Gar

Black
Drum

Schoolmaster
Snapper

Upsid
Dow
Jellyf

MANGROVE SWAMP MERMAIDS

Biscayne Bay, FL

Saltwater swamps are often dominated by mangrove trees. These specially adapted trees live their whole lives with their long "prop roots" sunk down underwater, forming dense, tangled thickets along subtropical coastlines.

Mangrove swamps are the nurseries of the ocean. Nearby coral reefs are great places to be an adult fish or mermaid, but they can be dangerous places to grow up, full of predators and rough water. Instead, many ocean mermaid naiads begin their lives in the shelter of mangrove roots.

Some mermaids choose to stay in the swamps after they're older, helping to raise baby fish and sea turtles. They've also been known to transplant mangrove seedlings, often attempting to repopulate groves that have been wiped out by shoreline buildings and seawalls.

BAYOU MERMAIDS

Atchafalaya River Basin, LA

A bayou is technically a slow-moving section of river that floods the surrounding lowlands, making them a challenge to categorize—they are usually a mixture of swamps, rivers, and floodplains all in one. Most frequently found in states that border the Gulf of Mexico, bayous can be freshwater or brackish, often extending out into saltwater marshes and mangrove swamps.

Bayou mermaids hold the distinction of reaching the largest sizes of any wetland mermaids. Being large has a drawback, however. Damming and draining of bayous have limited the extensive habitat mermaids of this size need to survive, and pollutant runoff has made some sections uninhabitable. Occasionally, mermaids of incredible size have been seen crawling across roads to reach water on the other side.

Alligator

BAYGALL BOG MERMAIDS
Big Thicket, TX

Baygalls are forest bogs. They show up as pockets of water left in floodplains after floods recede. Kept wet by underground seeps, baygalls are different from some other bogs because they're often completely covered by the forest canopy. Their name comes from two of the most common plants that grow there—sweet*bay* magnolia and *gall*berry holly. But there are a huge variety of other plants that love these bogs, including some of the most unusual in the country—carnivorous plants. Because bog soils are low in nutrients, these plants get most of their nutrients by "eating" insects, often by trapping them on sticky lures or making them slip into funnels filled with liquid that then digests them.

Bogs are buggy places, so mermaids have a special friendship with carnivorous plants. Mermaids happily cultivate and feed these *insectivorous* plants mosquitoes, midges, and flies that often cloud the surface of bogs. Perhaps unsurprisingly, bog mermaids themselves tend to be insectivores, as well.

Widow Skimmer

Bladderwort

Pitcher Plant

Sundew

Venus Flytr

Butterwort

60

Bluespotted Sunfish

FLOODPLAIN FOREST MERMAIDS
Congaree River, SC

Floodplain forests differ from swamps because they're not underwater all the time—only when a river rises past its banks to flood the surrounding area. During periods of high water, river mermaids, like those living in the Congaree River, can leave their usual course and swim leisurely between trunks of cypress and tupelo trees.

Floodplains are also home to *estivating* mermaids. Estivation is similar to hibernation, except it happens during droughts instead of winter. Rather than migrate with the receding water, these mermaids will settle down in the deep, damp mud and enter a state of torpor. The thick mud keeps them from drying out, letting them respirate through their skin. In this way, they can wait out the dry season and take to the water again when the floods return.

Moose

CREATURE FEATURE

Moose—These antlered herbivores are superb swimmers and divers. Their long legs let them wade through mucky environments, and their specialized nostrils can be sealed shut underwater, which means they can chew and swallow without lifting their heads above the surface!

KETTLE BOG MERMAIDS

Moose Bog, VT

The same glaciers that carved so many lakes in the United States also created many other types of unique landforms. Some of these are kettles, which are formed when chunks of ice break off a retreating glacier. As the block of ice melts, it deposits the rocks and sediment it was carrying, building up a ring around it and leaving a round, scooped hole in its place. When streams or rainwater fill this hole, it becomes a kettle lake or pond. Over time, kettles often become covered with floating plants, usually sphagnum moss, which form a spongy mat on top of the water.

It's in these mossy, acidic pools that you'll find bog mermaids, often hiding right under the mat itself. Because the water in bogs doesn't flow, the kettles have very low levels of oxygen. This means fish have trouble surviving in these waters, but mermaids have plenty of other animals to keep them company, from tiny frogs eating the plentiful insects to giant water-loving moose grazing on aquatic plants!

Sphagnum
Moss

POCOSIN MERMAIDS

Alligator River, NC

Pocosins are a type of shrub wetland, with dark, mucky peat soils kept wet by water seeping up from underground. They're found only in a few places near the coasts of South Carolina, North Carolina, and Virginia. What makes them so unusual is their high tolerance to wildfires—in fact, many of the plant species in pocosins, like the pond pine, rely on fire to help them spread. Their cones are kept shut by a sticky sap that only melts away when heated by fire, allowing them to spread their seeds. Sometimes, pocosin fires are so intense that they burn right down into the peat, which creates hollows for new ponds. This is a good example of how fire is an important natural part of many landscapes.

Mermaids live a touch-and-go life in pocosins. They are similar to their floodplain cousins in how they rely on the damp soil to protect them from drought and wildfire. If things get too dry, or a fire approaches, mermaids will quickly gather their aquatic friends together and burrow down in the mud.

Pine Barrens
Tree Frog

Dusky
Salamander

Chiricahua Leopard Frog

Huachuca
Water Umbel

Gila
Topminnow

CIÉNEGA MERMAIDS
Cloverdale, NM

When you think of the desert, you probably picture someplace dry and sandy, perhaps with cacti and rock mesas marching into the horizon. The desert Southwest is indeed a dry, dusty place, but up until the past few hundred years, it was also a landscape dotted with freshwater marshes called ciénegas. These soggy, flooded meadows often stretched across valley floors, fed by underground seeps and springs. Nowadays, after many years of being drained, diverted, and trampled by livestock, most ciénegas are just trickling streams rather than wide marshy meadows.

Mermaids in ciénegas, while rare, can still be found in some of the few undamaged desert wetlands left. They are small, hardy species adept at moving through spongy vegetation and grassy waterways. Despite their shrinking habitats, ciénega mermaids very rarely abandon their homes—crawling away into the desert is just too risky.

FREEZING WETLAND MERMAIDS
Prairie Potholes, SD

Mermaids in rivers or lakes have options for survival when winter freezes hit, but what do mermaids in wetlands do? Some, perhaps, can migrate or shelter in deep water, but some only have access to shallow pools and wet meadows. In the Prairie Pothole Region of the Dakotas, for example, there are thousands of glacier-carved ponds, but they're often surrounded by wide grasslands. What do mermaids do when these freeze over?

Something amazing, it turns out. Mermaids in these freezing wetlands have adapted with the incredible ability to freeze solid but not die. When winter comes, much like their estivating cousins in floodplain forests, they settle down under some nice mud and let their bodies freeze. Their heartbeats and breathing slow and then stop, and ice forms in their blood and around their internal organs. While this would kill most animals, their bodies produce high amounts of sugar that acts as a kind of "antifreeze" for their cells, keeping them alive. As spring arrives, they thaw and head back out into their favorite pools, good as new.

CREATURE FEATURE

Wood Frogs—These incredible frogs are masters of cold environments and are the only frog found above the Arctic Circle. When frozen, they appear like rock-solid, frog-shaped statues. In the coldest parts of their range, they can survive temperatures as low as -50 degrees Fahrenheit and can freeze for up to eight months!

Wood Frog

67

COASTAL WATER
MERMAIDS

WHERE THE OCEANS MEET LAND

With a few exceptions, all lakes, rivers, and wetlands ultimately drain into the sea. Coasts are the places where land and fresh water reach the salt water of the ocean. These can be gentle sandy beaches or jagged rocky cliffs—and both of these types of environments support different types of plants, animals, and mermaids. Coastlines are busy, buzzing places—most of the animals in the oceans stick to shorelines, creating communities not unlike cities on land, full of strange, wonderful creatures.

Coastal mermaids are perhaps the most famous of all mermaids—people throughout the ages have spied them (or thought they have) perched on rocks, lounging on beaches, or swimming just under the waves. And coastal mermaids certainly earn their well-known reputation. The largest groups of mermaids congregate along coasts, and they come in an endless variety. Some are flashy and sporty, fond of playing in the expanses of sunny water. Others are shy and secretive, preferring the shelter of crevices and plant beds. Because of the wide variety of coastal habitats, mermaids of all kinds can find a place that suits them.

When you are exploring coasts to look for mermaids, you can ask yourself these questions:

- Is the shore here rocky or sandy?
- Is there a big difference between high and low tide, or is it relatively small?
- What kinds of plants might grow in the water?
- Are there lots of buildings along the shore? How might that impact mermaids?
- Do I know how the currents or seasons affect this area?
- If I were a mermaid, what might I like about this habitat? What might be a problem?

SANDY COAST MERMAIDS
Padre Island, TX

Pushed, pulled, smoothed, and sculpted by wind and waves, sandy shorelines are constantly changing. Formed by eroding rock or, in some cases, fish poop (some fish nibble on coral and then poop out sand!), these beaches are the front lines for protecting inland habitats like marshes and rivers. Despite the appearance of being deserts, sandy coasts are teeming with life, both in the water and in the sand itself.

Sandy coast mermaids spend their time cruising the warm, shallow waters or relaxing on the beach. Similar to the sleek, sporty mermaids in the sunlit zone of the ocean, these mermaids are athletic and fast. Life isn't all about playing in the surf, though. Many mermaids take special care of an important part of sandy beaches—sea turtle nests. Mermaids often swim with female turtles coming to shore to nest, and later join them on the beach to protect nests from poaching by hungry birds, reptiles, and mammals.

Ring-Billed Gull

CREATURE FEATURE

Kemp's Ridley Sea Turtle—The smallest and most critically endangered sea turtles, they nest on only a few beaches in the Gulf of Mexico.

Kemp's Ridley Sea Turtle

Manatee

Horseshoe
Crab

SEAGRASS MEADOW MERMAIDS
Everglades, FL

Picture a rolling prairie of lush green grasses, waving gently, and over the horizon comes a majestic . . . manatee? Welcome to the seagrass meadows. Mermaids here spend their days basking and playing in the warm shallows. They're highly social, and often have large groups of friends and family extending into the surrounding mangrove swamps, coral reefs, and estuaries. Because of this, they're tolerant of different levels of salinity, meaning they can socialize with their relatives in saltwater reefs or brackish river deltas before cruising back home to snooze amid the lush grasses.

SEAGRASS VS. SEAWEED

Seagrass is different from seaweed. Seagrass is a type of flowering plant with roots that extract nutrients from the sediment. Seaweed, however, is a type of algae. Instead of roots, it anchors itself with "holdfasts" and extracts nutrients from the water.

Harlequin
Ducks

ROCKY COAST MERMAIDS

Three Arch Rocks, OR

Watch a wave crashing against a rocky shore and it's easy to see the power at play in these landscapes. Rocky coasts are battered by wind, waves, and, in many cases, ice—as well as sculpted by tectonic activity like earthquakes. These forces grind small sediment like sand away, leaving dramatic landscapes like cliffs, arches, sea stacks, and sea caves.

Water here can be turbulent and unpredictable, and currents can be fearsomely strong, so mermaids along rocky coasts need to be powerful swimmers. Many have strong or overlarge pectoral fins to help them maneuver and tall dorsal fins to keep them steady in racing tides. Pounding waves mean the water is often cloudy, so it's important for mermaids to be able to navigate without relying on eyesight. Just like bats and whales, mermaids use echolocation to get an accurate "picture" of their surroundings when visibility is low. Clicking, bubble-blowing, whistling, and their famous ethereal singing are all ways that mermaids communicate and find their way through rough water.

KELP FOREST MERMAIDS
Monterey Bay, CA

Usually found in cold, nutrient-rich water, kelps are fast, hardy growers—some can grow between one to two feet a day! Just like a forest on land, these underwater groves of giant seaweed house diverse populations of grazers and predators and, of course, mermaids.

Kelp forest mermaids are especially playful, much like the sea otters they share their habitats with. Quick and clever, they are often seen darting in and out of the thick, waving stalks and creating colorful baubles to wear. Mermaids in these forests play an important role in maintaining the health of the ecosystem. Kelp is incredibly strong, but these mighty plants can be felled by tiny creatures. Spiky sea urchins roam the ocean floor and can graze through the kelp's *holdfasts*, or anchors, killing vast stretches of forests and leaving behind "urchin barrens." Fortunately, mermaids in these forests have developed a fondness for making crowns out of urchins, especially the brightly colored purple urchins.

Purple Sea Urchin

Sea Otter

California Sheephead

Garibaldi

Giant Kelp

Nudibranch—Pronounced NOOD-i-brangk, these alien-looking creatures, some-times called sea slugs, are shell-less mollusks renowned for their phenomenal colors and whimsical tentacle-like projections. Because they lack protective shells, many absorb the toxic properties of prey they eat, such as stinging cells from jellyfish!

Salmon-Gilled
Nudibranch

Rockweed

76

Acadian
Hermit Crab

White Atlantic
Cadlina

Spiny Sun
Star

Periwinkle
Snails

TIDE POOL MERMAIDS
Mount Desert Island, ME

L ife along the coast is impacted by a force that's literally out of this world—the
gravitational pull of Earth's moon. As the earth spins, the moon pulls on the
water that's facing it, which causes regular fluctuations in water levels known as
tides. Along the shore of Maine, those tides can rise and fall as much as twelve feet
in just a few hours. When the tide recedes, it leaves behind tide pools—pockets of
water that can host a colorful circus of astounding invertebrates . . . and mermaids.

Tide pool mermaids enjoy making new friends. They have to—their habitats
change drastically several times a day, always bringing and carrying away new
organisms. Mermaids and their fellow tide pool creatures have to be able to adapt
to two extremes—the risk of drying out at low tide and the force of the waves as
they come crashing back in. Many mermaids will squeeze down into wet crevices
with animals like sea stars, or scoot after the receding water like crabs. A hardy
few will stay in the high, exposed pools and drape themselves in damp rockweed
as they await the return of the tide. To bear the crashing waves, some mermaids
wedge themselves among mussels and oysters anchored to the rocks, apparently
enjoying the thrill of the oncoming surf. All of this activity happens twice a day.
Life as a tide pool mermaid can be exhausting, to say the least.

CORAL REEF MERMAIDS

Papahānaumokuākea, HI

A riot of color, sound, and movement, coral reefs are the dazzling metropolitan cities of the ocean. Coral polyps—tiny squishy animals—grow hard calcium skeletons in all kinds of shapes and sizes, forming the foundation of reef communities, like buildings in a city. Huge arrays of mermaids, fish, invertebrates, and marine mammals flock to these reefs in search of food, mates, habitats, or just to be part of the most vibrant social scene in the ocean.

Mermaids in coral reefs are so diverse, they're almost impossible to summarize. Some are only visitors, passing through to socialize and refuel as they make their way through the open ocean, while others are full-time residents. Some like the rowdy nightlife among roving whitetip sharks, while others prefer watching the action while tucked in among the coral with moray eels or sailing along the fringes with green sea turtles. But whether they're gregarious or solitary, visitors or residents, all coral reef mermaids share a common love for jewelry and decoration. Reef mermaids fashion

Dragon
Moray Eel

Pennant
Butterflyfish

Crown-
of-Thorns
Starfish

the most elaborate and colorful accessories of any species, many times recruiting living creatures to pose as adornments—crowns of harlequin shrimp, garlands of spiky urchins, swathes of vibrant starfish, plus all manner of pearls, pebbles, and bits of coral strung into necklaces unparalleled by any other population.

Despite being made of hard stony skeletons, coral reefs are fragile communities and are threatened by rising temperatures, ocean acidification, and pollution runoff. Reef mermaids may be a fun-loving group, but they also work hard to care for their precious habitat. Many have gardens where they cultivate baby corals to replace ones lost to bleaching or breakage. Others do the tiring, never-ending work of removing invasive algae and trash, while still others care for nurseries of native creatures.

Staghorn Coral

Harlequin Shrimp

Red Pencil Urchin

Table Coral

Spectacled Parrotfish

MERMAID ARCHITECTURE

Mermaid architecture can range from single dwellings in natural caves to banks of roots, all the way to sprawling underwater cities with towering spires, arches, and spirals. Like their penchant for jewelry (see page 54), mermaids enjoy growing, sculpting, and decorating their homes with whatever materials are available to them.

Freshwater mermaids often rely on stone and wood to build their architecture, often soliciting the help of animal specialists. Beavers can help cut and shape wood, and muskrats can help gather weeds and grass for weaving. But there are even more unexpected freshwater builders that mermaids take cues from. Many small minnow species, such as river chub and stone rollers, are accomplished rock-movers and can help mermaids gather pebbles for building materials. Aquatic insects like caddis flies build their own portable houses by gluing together tiny rocks and plant fragments with silk. It's thought that observing these insects taught mermaids how to mortar their own stone structures.

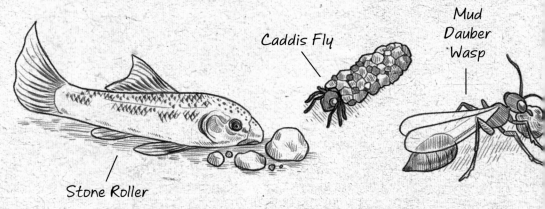

Caddis Fly

Mud Dauber Wasp

Stone Roller

For wetland mermaids, the goal of architecture is always to maximize moisture. Mud, clay, weeds, and roots are used to full effect to protect mermaids from drying out during fluctuating water levels. Some mermaids follow the lead of alligators and dig shallow holes that hold water during dry seasons. Wetland mermaids are the most accomplished at working with clay, often copying the sculpting skills of animals like mud dauber wasps to create shelters that remain cool and damp inside.

The crown jewels of saltwater mermaid architecture are coral reefs. Reef mermaids have long and illustrious histories of growing and training living coral into fabulous grottoes and palaces. These corals and their related cousins—sea sponges, sea squirts, sea fans, hydroids, and bryozoans—can be cultivated much like a garden and grown into beautiful structures. Some types of coral are even employed for their defense mechanisms, such as fire coral and do-not-touch-me sponges, which deliver a painful burn to skin when accidentally touched. Not only do these coral gardens create habitats for mermaids and marine life alike—they also help regrow reefs that have been damaged or destroyed by climate change.

CAPE MERMAIDS
Cape Cod, MA

Along a shoreline, capes are places where the land juts out into the sea. They have a big impact on how the ocean currents move—and therefore, what kinds of animals are found there. The ecosystems on either side of a cape can be very different, even though just a few miles of land separates them. At Cape Cod, Massachusetts, for example, the cool Maine Current flows down from the north, while the warmer Gulf Stream flows up from the south. The water temperature on either side of the cape can differ by as much as ten degrees Fahrenheit.

Because of the way capes affect currents and water temperatures, they often act as barriers to ocean life, serving as the southernmost point many northern species can comfortably travel, while the opposite goes for species traveling north. This makes capes traditional meeting places for coastal mermaids. They frequently travel to meet in the mingling currents, swapping stories, songs, and accessories from southern and northern waters.

Bull Shark

Right Whale

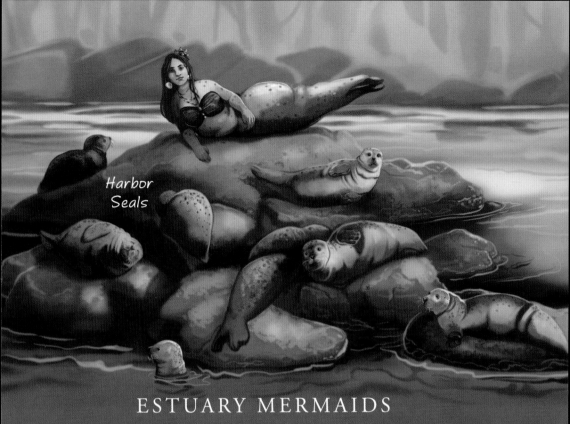

Harbor
Seals

ESTUARY MERMAIDS
Narragansett Bay, RI

An estuary is a place where salt water and fresh water meet, creating *brackish* water. Life in estuaries is constantly changing, as temperature, depth, saltiness, and currents fluctuate over the course of hours, days, and seasons.

Estuary mermaids are well adapted to the changing nature of their habitat. They often have favorite resting spots above high tide lines, and they have no problem moving between salt and fresh water. But like all mermaids, they can't survive without clean water, and in estuaries, this can be a problem. Estuaries are often prime spots for shipping lanes, factories, and commercial fisheries. What's more, rivers flush all the pollution they've gathered upstream into estuaries. Mermaids have long worked to keep their beloved estuary bays and inlets clean, collecting trash, tending beds of filter feeders like oysters and clams, and finding homes for animals displaced by human use.

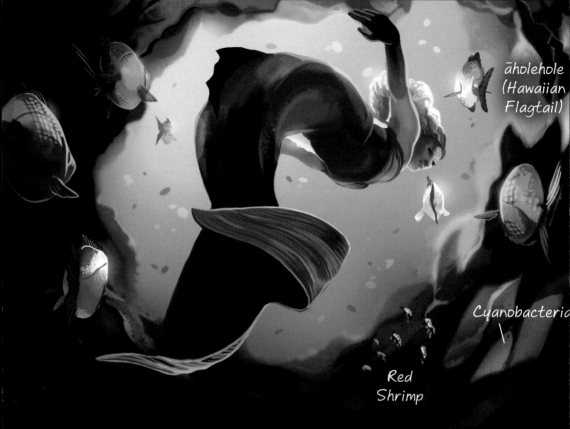

āholehole
(Hawaiian
Flagtail)

Cyanobacteria

Red
Shrimp

ANCHIALINE POOL MERMAIDS
Cape Kīnaʻu, HI

Anchialine (pronounced AN-key-ah-lin) pools are unusual coastal pools that have an underground connection to the ocean. They exist in large numbers on the volcanic islands of Hawaiʻi. Some are tiny and only connect to the ocean through cracks in the rocks, but others are large and have long underwater sea caves through old lava tubes. They are usually brackish near the surface and saltier in their depths, because fresh water is less dense than salt water and floats on top of it.

Mermaids in these pools are similar to those in freshwater karst systems—while it may seem like they live in just a small pool, they actually have access to long underwater tunnels. Explorers by nature, they eagerly brave unknown passages and the unusual creatures that live in them.

FJORD MERMAIDS

Kenai Fjords, AK

Powerful coastal glaciers carve steep, narrow valleys that flood with seawater, creating fjords (pronounced fyords). As the glacier retreats, its fresh water mixes with the seawater to create an estuary environment.

Fjord estuary mermaids are frequently migratory, spending the summers in these cold waters. Wintertime can often find them heading back down the coast. But not all—there's a species of porpoise mermaid that thrives year-round in these deep, glacial-fed inlets. The cold weather doesn't slow them down one bit—they're an especially fun-loving species, fond of plowing through the surface water and kicking up spray above them.

CREATURE FEATURE

Dall's Porpoise—Sometimes reported as tiny orcas, Dall's porpoises are year-round residents of Alaskan fjords, diving deep into the steep underwater valleys to feed on squid, crustaceans, and fish. Despite their food often being several hundred feet underwater, they like to play at the surface, swimming extra fast and creating a distinctive "rooster tail" spray with their dorsal fins!

Common Murres

Dall's Porpoise

85

FROZEN COAST MERMAIDS

Beaufort Sea, AK

Up in the Arctic Circle are oceans that only thaw for a few weeks each year, under skies that can see sun at midnight in the summer and darkness at noon in the winter. Here, *fast ice* clings to the shoreline, while *drift ice* moves with the wind and currents. Sheets of ice fracture, blocks of it break away, thin sheets of it pile up, and slush can coat the surface of the sea. These waters are alive with the movement of ice.

These are the playgrounds of Arctic mermaids, who thrive in the icy waters. Many are pure white, to camouflage amid the ice from predators like killer whales and polar bears. Almost half of their body weight is blubber, which insulates them from the cold. Unlike some other mermaids, they have no fins on their backs, which lets them swim under the ice more easily. Arctic mermaids rely on good ice cover to protect themselves—as our climate changes and more ice melts, this has become a problem for these cold-water mermaids, who now find themselves facing larger and larger stretches of open water.

Beluga Whale

Arctic Cod

OPEN OCEAN
MERMAIDS

LAYERS OF LIFE

A way from the coastline stretches the open ocean, a place full of life, and yet so vast it can seem like a watery desert. Oceans cover almost three-quarters of Earth's surface, but they're the least explored places on the globe. Mermaids who live here range from the instantly recognizable to the most mysterious and least known in the world.

A good way to explore the different kinds of mermaids in the ocean is to divide the water up into layers. These are called zones, and their differences rely on the amount of sunlight able to penetrate the water, which affects the temperature and amount of plant life present. Most mermaids in the ocean occupy the top two zones, but some of the most unusual species are found down in the depths. You won't find as many specific locations listed for these zones in the following pages, because many of these mermaids and animals appear throughout the ocean.

When you are exploring the open ocean to look for mermaids, you can ask yourself these questions:

- Are there underwater features that might impact life in this area?
- Do I know what kind of fishing happens in this area? How might this impact mermaids?
- What adaptations might mermaids have to survive in this area?
- What kinds of predators live in this area? How might mermaids protect themselves from them?
- If I were a mermaid, what might I like about this habitat? What might be a problem?

Ocean Sunfish

SUNLIT ZONE MERMAIDS
The Gulf of Mexico

E ndless blue water, the flashing of silvery fish, a glimpse of dolphin spray or whale flukes . . . this is the open ocean that most people know. This sunny slice of surface waters is home to most of the mermaids and other animals in the ocean.

The fastest of all mermaids live in the sunlit zone. Many have giant dorsal fins to stabilize them, while others have miniature fins instead to reduce drag in the water. Some sunlit mermaids can also change color, flashing different patterns to confuse prey. Life isn't all about action, though. Plenty of mermaids enjoy the sunlit zone for the ability to simply bask in the warm rays, drifting leisurely wherever the currents take them.

CREATURE FEATURE

Ocean Sunfish—One of the strangest fish in the ocean might be the ocean sunfish, also known as a mola. Shaped like a giant disk, they're the largest and heaviest bony fish, weighing almost as much as a pickup truck! Despite their giant size, they are peaceful creatures, eating mostly jellyfish and drifting lazily just under the surface.

SARGASSUM DRIFT MERMAIDS

The Sargasso Sea

Up in the sunlit zone, baby sea turtles and fish are vulnerable to all kinds of predators from both below and above. Many find refuge in floating rafts of sargassum, a seaweed equipped with little air-filled bladders that let it bob near the surface and gather into thick, tangled mats. Part of the Atlantic Ocean has so much sargassum that it's known as the Sargasso Sea.

Some animals live their whole lives in these drifting havens, including a unique species of mermaid. With tails and hair perfectly camouflaged for their weedy golden-brown environment, they shepherd baby animals traveling through the open ocean. The seaweed rafts also provide an easy mode of transportation, as mermaids can relax in their tangled shelter, or even on top, to float wherever the current takes them.

Sargassum
Fish

Loggerhead
Sea Turtle

93

Feather Duster
Worms

Barrel
Sponges

Pom-Pom
Anemone

Rosy Rockfish

Hydrocoral

94

CONTINENTAL SHELF MERMAIDS
Cordell Bank, CA

The ocean floor isn't just an empty flat plain—throughout the water are undersea mountains and cliffs that rise toward the surface. These obstructions force deep, cold currents upward, which bring nutrients, like billowing clouds of phytoplankton and zooplankton, with them. These can create oases in the middle of the ocean that draw life from all over, much like a pool of water in a desert. On the Cordell Bank off the coast of California, the edge of the continental shelf forces great clouds of nutrients over an underwater island, creating a colorful, energetic community.

Mermaids in these areas are famous builders. Like their warm-water cousins on the tropical reefs of Hawai'i and Florida, they enjoy tinkering with their colorful surroundings, but perhaps because of the strength of the currents and the more isolated nature of their habitat, they tend to put their efforts into building structures rather than jewelry. Some of the most stunning undersea architecture can be found in places like the Cordell Bank, where mermaids spend years lovingly tending corals and sponges to grow in intricate arches and grottoes.

Phytoplankton

Zooplankton

CREATURE FEATURE

Phytoplankton—Microscopic plants that drift with the current.

Zooplankton—Tiny animals, including krill and the larvae of crabs, jellyfish, and fish. Because they don't photosynthesize like phytoplankton do, they can live at greater depths.

Swordfish

TWILIGHT ZONE MERMAIDS

Below the bright, warm sunlit zone lies the twilight zone. While some sunlight penetrates this far, it's not enough for plants to grow. Animals here drift through the gloom or dive down from the surface, searching for the thick clouds of zooplankton that drift like soup in the dimmer water.

An unusual type of mermaid lives here, one that makes the trip between the twilight and sunlit zones each night. These are called vertical migrators, and they spend their days down in the cool, dim waters of the twilight zone. As night falls, they rise up into the warmer waters of the sunlit zone. They're following their food sources—squids and jellyfish that are in turn chasing zooplankton. This makes vertical migrating mermaids nocturnal, resting in the twilight zone during the day and becoming active at night, which allows them to conserve energy.

MIDNIGHT ZONE MERMAIDS

Darkness becomes complete. Temperature drops. This is the midnight zone, where no light from the surface penetrates at all. It's bigger than the twilight and sunlit zones above it, but it has far fewer animals. While some of these creatures are full-time residents of the midnight zone, this is also as deep as the strongest surface mermaids and other animals, like sperm whales, elephant seals, and Cuvier's beaked whales, can dive.

Diving mermaids swim to these depths to reach squid and fish. Though they're not adapted to stay this deep permanently, they do have incredible ways to survive the intense pressure and frigid temperature. Their bodies are streamlined so they can descend extra fast, and they can actually slow down their heart rate to keep from using too much oxygen. Before they dive, they blow out all the air in their lungs, which helps them dive faster and resist the crushing pressure that would kill many other organisms.

Cuvier's
Beaked Whale

BIOLUMINESCENT MERMAIDS
Deep Sea

Have you ever seen fireflies blinking at night? Travel into the ocean depths, and you would probably see something similar: flashes and trails of light glowing eerily in the gloom. This *bioluminescence* is made by a chemical reaction inside some creatures' bodies and can be used to lure prey, attract a mate, or scare away danger. Over 70 percent of deep-sea animals can make their own light.

BIOLUMINESCENCE:
light produced by living things.

Bioluminescent mermaids come in all shapes and sizes. Some have bodies that glow all the way through, while others have twinkling patterns. Some have eyes that shine like headlights, and some have long, glowing lures that trail behind them.

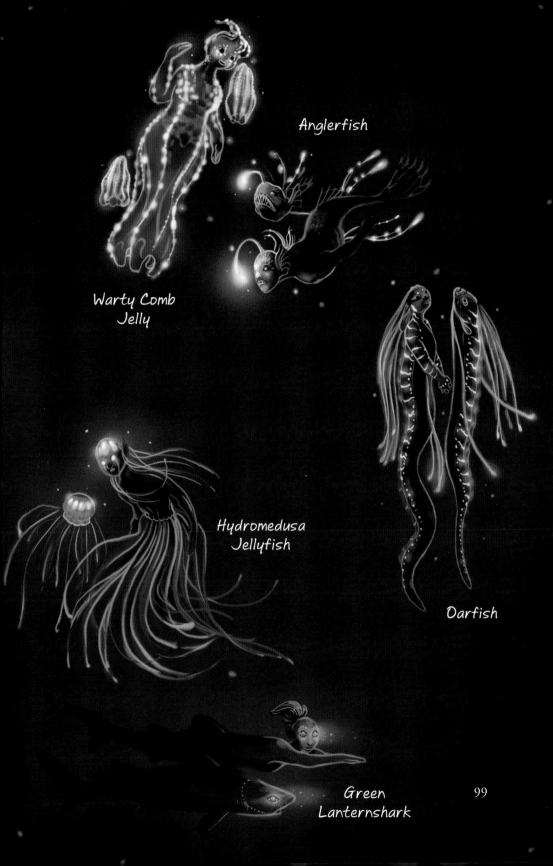

Anglerfish

Warty Comb
Jelly

Hydromedusa
Jellyfish

Oarfish

Green
Lanternshark

99

MERMAID GIGANTISM

How big might something grow if there was nothing to stop it from growing? In a word, *gigantic*. The biggest mermaids in the world are found down in the midnight zone, along with other massive sea life like giant squid. These mermaids spend their lives floating in an open sea, rarely encountering land, the surface, or the ocean floor at all. Some can grow to be over seventy feet long—almost two school buses put together!

At these depths, food is scarce and the water is icy cold, so giant mermaids swim slowly, almost lazily, to conserve energy. They have massive eyes to help them see in the pitch black, and they nearly always produce light. They live solitary lives and can live over a hundred years, often going many years between encountering any other mermaids.

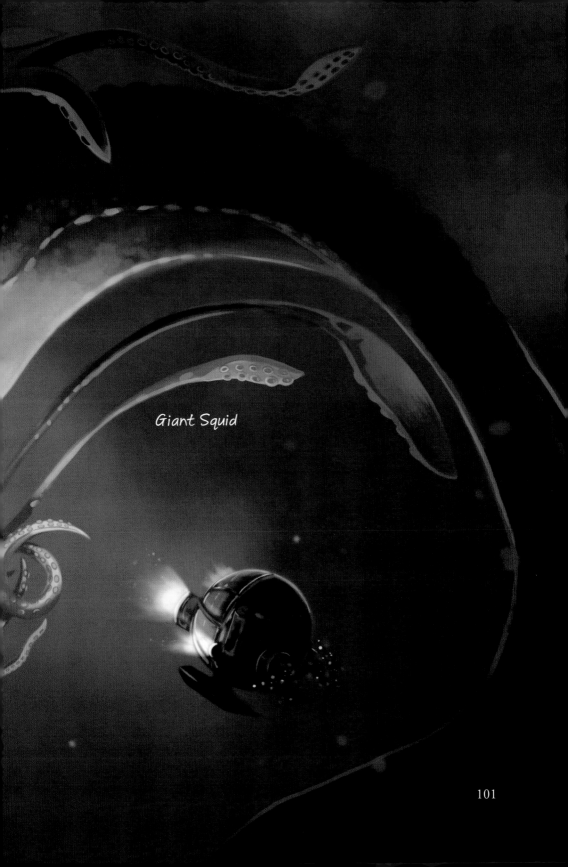

Giant Squid

HOW HUMANS EXPLORE THE DEEP

The deep ocean is one of the most difficult places for humans to study on earth, but that hasn't stopped us from trying for thousands of years. Driven by curiosity, humans have pushed the limits of their bodies and technology to plumb the depths of the sea.

16.4 feet: The depth of an Olympic diving pool
Most swimming pools require a depth of at least eight feet in order to safely use a diving board.

160 feet: Typical SCUBA depth limit
Scuba divers use a variety of gear to move and breathe underwater. Most recreational divers stay above 60 feet.

SCUBA GEAR

426 feet: Deepest unassisted free dive
Free divers rely only on their ability to hold their breath, rather than using a tank of air. They often use fins and can stay underwater for almost four minutes.

702 feet: Deepest weighted free dive

To reach these depths, a free diver uses a weight to help them descend and a balloon-like float to help them rise back to the surface.

1,090 feet: Deepest competitive SCUBA dive

Ultra-deep scuba diving is considered anything beyond 660 feet and is highly dangerous due to extreme pressure and cold temperatures. Even with advanced training, gear, and physical fitness, only a tiny number of divers ever go this deep.

2,300 feet: Deepest limit for atmospheric diving suit

An atmospheric diving suit is like an underwater space suit that's monitored and assisted by a crew at the surface. While a person in this kind of protective exo-skeleton can go deeper than a scuba diver, they have limited mobility.

14,800 feet: Typical limit for research deep-dives

These deep-sea submarines are crewed by small teams of pilots and researchers and have made huge advances in human knowledge about the dark zones of the ocean.

35,858 feet: Deep-sea submersibles in the Mariana Trench

Fewer than ten people in the world have reached the deepest point in the ocean, called the Challenger Deep, part of the Mariana Trench in the Pacific Ocean. This area is so deep that if you flipped Mount Everest upside down, its summit would still be seven thousand feet short of the bottom.

ABYSSAL ZONE MERMAIDS

Welcome to the abyssal zone—the very bottom of the ocean. This harsh, distant environment can be anywhere from four to seven miles below the surface. The mermaids and animals that live down here are the most mysterious and the least understood of any species.

It might be surprising to know that there are coral reefs down here, just like the famous, colorful ones up in warm coastal water. Unlike those bright, busy coastal reefs, though, these are ghostly and quiet. Everything from the coral to the mermaids that live here are pale and bleached of color. These mermaids never see any light except the pale glow emitted by other creatures, so their eyes are huge. Their bodies are built to withstand immense pressure from the miles of ocean above them.

Despite this alien environment, mermaids here still have roles to play in their habitats. Some guide scavenging animals to useful debris that has found its long way down from the surface. Others gather rubbish that has drifted down to the ocean floor—all the trash that has reached its final resting place.

Chain
Catshark

Giant
Isopod

Hatchetfish

OCEAN TRENCH MERMAIDS

Among the rugged underwater mountains, slopes, and reefs are trenches that plunge for miles and miles, just like canyons on land. These are the deepest places on our planet. Exploring these extreme depths is as challenging as exploring outer space, and yet scientists have evidence of mermaids living down here. A slow wave of a giant tail, a glimpse of a webbed hand, the shine of distant bioluminescence—these are the few clues we have of these deepest of all mermaids.

What do *you* think they might be like?

105

EXTREME AND UNLIKELY MERMAID HABITATS

LIFE AT THE LIMIT

This book has shown habitats that most people are familiar with—nearly everyone can picture a stream, or a lake, or a beach. But there are some mermaids who live in places that are not only surprising, but seem like the last places anything could possibly survive. Boiling water, blocks of ice, water so salty it pickles everything in it . . . could anything live in these kinds of habitats?

The answer, as you've probably guessed, is yes!

Mermaids have been found in places that not even other vertebrates like fish or mammals can survive. Organisms that live in these kinds of habitats are called *extremophiles*. *Phile* means "lover"—thus, these are mermaids who love extreme conditions, like very high or low temperatures, unusual types of water, or even human-made structures. Finding mermaids in these unlikely places is a reminder that life on earth is ancient, adaptive, and absolutely mind-blowing.

When you are exploring unlikely habitats to look for mermaids, you can ask yourself these questions:

- What makes this habitat extreme or unusual?
- What adaptations would a mermaid need to survive here?
- How might a mermaid move around this environment?
- Are there other organisms that can survive here, too?
- If I were a mermaid, what might I like about this habitat? What might be a problem?

Yellow
Monkeyflower

Thermophile
Bacteria

HOT SPRING MERMAIDS
Yellowstone National Park, WY, ID, MT

Hot springs are pools of super-hot water, heated deep underground by chambers of magma. While hot springs exist in several places around the world, most of them are found in Yellowstone National Park, which has thousands of hissing, steaming, and bubbling thermal features.

The heat-loving mermaids that live in these springs are called *thermophile* mermaids (*thermo* means "heat"). They never venture above the surface for long—even on hot days, the air is too chilly for them! They thrive alongside tiny thermophile bacteria, which give the water its vibrant colors. Thermophile mermaids' tails can change color to match the temperature of the water they're in. Down in the hottest depths, they turn bright sapphire and indigo, while up in the cooler (but still hot!) water, they may appear daffodil yellow, neon orange, ruby red, or emerald green.

HYDROTHERMAL VENT MERMAIDS

Hydrothermal vents spew superheated, mineral-rich water into the ocean. When this water hits the frigid temperatures of the deep sea, the minerals solidify and form towering chimneys that become home to alien creatures like tube worms, giant clams, blind crabs, and even eels and octopuses.

Mermaids at hydrothermal vents rely on the energy produced by the vents, which fuels the thick bacterial mats that feed the other creatures clustered around these chimneys. This makes them some of the only mermaids in the world that don't rely on sunlight to fuel their food chain. Because of this specialized lifestyle, most vent mermaids don't move very far away from their particular habitat.

CHEMOSYNTHESIS: *creating energy from chemicals, rather than from sunlight (that is, photosynthesis).*

Giant Tube Worm

Clams

Vent Octopus

SALT LAKE MERMAIDS
Great Salt Lake, UT

Landlocked and much smaller than any sea, salt lakes can actually be more salty than the ocean—the Great Salt Lake in Utah, for example, is five to ten times saltier than anything you'd find at the coast. These kinds of lakes form when rivers flow down into a basin, but none flow out of it. The only way out for the water is through evaporation, which leaves salts behind. This means salt lakes are always getting saltier!

Mermaids in salt lakes are highly specialized to withstand the briny, super-salty water without getting pickled in it. While most creatures are adapted to keep salt out of their cells, mermaids in hypersaline water have cells that are just as salty as the water around them. These salt-loving extremophiles are known as *halophiles*.

The Great Salt Lake is unusual in another way—it's split through the middle by a railroad bridge. While some freshwater rivers pour into the southern section, there are no rivers in the northern section, which makes that water saltier than the south. While the southern waters are an expected bluish color, the north can be a bright bubblegum pink! That's because the tiny halophile critters in the extra-salty water are pink themselves—and so are the mermaids.

Eared Grebe

Brine Shrimp

Chimaera

Mussels

BRINE POOLS
Gulf of Mexico

Down on the ocean floor are places where ancient salt beds occasionally break through the sediments above. This salt dissolves and creates pockets of super-salty water. Because this water is heavier than the rest of the seawater, it remains on the ocean floor in its own little pool.

If a mermaid were to try to dive into this hyper-salty pool, she would float on the top, because the water below is so dense. However, she wouldn't try this, because the water in the pools is so salty and laden with other chemicals that it's dangerous to almost any animal that might come in contact with it. This makes brine pools one of the few aquatic habitats that mermaids don't inhabit. Most only visit brine pools temporarily, perhaps to collect mussels.

Unless . . . there *is* something down there?

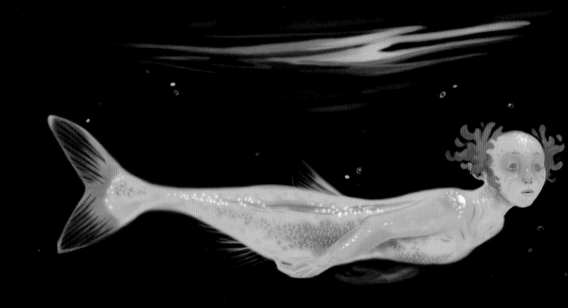

CAVE MERMAIDS

Fern Cave, AL

Deep underground, there are rivers and lakes that never see sunlight or feel the wind. These are cave waters—quiet, dark, cold, and full of mysteries.

Perhaps the strangest feature of many cave mermaids is that their eyes are exceptionally tiny. Thousands of years of evolution away from any light source has made eyesight unnecessary. These mermaids interact with their environment with the help of their lateral lines, which let them sense vibrations and currents in the water. They keep their frilly pink external gills their whole lives, even after they've become adults, which means they remain completely aquatic, similar to cave salamanders.

Between their missing eyes and ghostly appearance, these mermaids can seem spooky. But they are harmless and usually shy, and they have a fondness for gentle percussion instruments made from pebbles or snail shells.

GLACIER CAVE MERMAIDS

Mendenhall Glacier, AK

Glaciers are riddled with endless holes, crevasses, and caves that are always changing. Running water flows through many of these, carving out new paths and breaking old ones apart. Temperature changes mean chunks of ice can fall from the ceiling or cause the whole thing to collapse altogether. Combine this with the melting caused by climate change and glacier caves can be downright deadly places to call home.

And yet, mermaids will sometimes live in them. Whether drawn by the solitude, pure waters, ethereal beauty, or some other ancient reason, glacier mermaids can occasionally be seen sliding into deep blue crevasses or disappearing down waterfalls that fall into *moulins*, or wells in the tops of glaciers.

POLYNYA MERMAIDS
Chukchi Sea, AK

The frozen seas of the Arctic may seem like an already tough place to be a mermaid, but some icy habitats are even harsher than others, such as polynyas, which are stretches of open water completely surrounded by sea ice. They form when wind or water currents keep patches of water from freezing over, and they're some of the trickiest places in the world for an ocean creature to make a living.

Polynyas are vital for many air-breathing sea animals like whales and seals. Without access to the open air, these animals would drown, and without access to the sea, they become easy prey for polar bears. But sometimes, if the ice moves or freezes too quickly, an animal can get stuck inside one tiny polynya, unable to make the long trip to find another breathing hole.

There are several different kinds of Arctic mermaids, but some are experts at thriving in polynyas. Many will take up residence with a pod of whales that has become trapped overwinter, helping to keep the ice open so the animals can breathe.

Bowhead
Whale

Other mermaids scout out routes to open water and guide stranded animals safely out of the ice. When no routes are available, some mermaids will take it upon themselves to simply wait out the winter and keep the trapped animal company. This practice has led to the songs of polynya mermaids becoming some of the longest known to all merfolk, as heard by only a few fortunate ice fishers.

CREATURE FEATURE

Bowhead Whale—The bowhead whale is the only whale that lives year-round in the Arctic, and it can break through up to a foot of ice with its head. It has the largest mouth in the animal kingdom but eats only copepods—tiny crustaceans about the size of a grain of rice!

DESERT POOL MERMAIDS
Ash Meadows, NV

Peek into tiny pools and creeks scattered throughout the Mojave Desert and you may spy some of the rarest mermaids in the world. These desert mermaids and the fish they swim with have adapted to a harsh life in hot water, low oxygen, and high salinity—conditions that would be fatal to most other species. Because of how hot and dry the desert is, they're unable to crawl overland to new water sources like some other mermaids. Mermaids like these that are cut off from any other suitable water are the most vulnerable species to changes in their habitats. Changes to water levels, temperature, or food sources could send these species to extinction in the blink of an eye, after thousands of years of survival.

Pupfish

Red-Tailed Pennant

SWIMMING POOL MERMAIDS
Phoenix Metro Area, AZ

Our country used to be an interconnected land of wetlands, lakes, rivers, and coastlines. Modern development has chopped up this mosaic into pieces, draining wetlands, diverting rivers, and building fences, houses, and roads along shorelines. Mermaids and other animals aren't able to move as freely throughout old connected waterways as they once did. When faced with these challenges, some will adapt and take advantage of whatever water source is available to them, and in many urban backyards and city parks, this means swimming pools.

Swimming pools are not ideal places for mermaids—the chemicals used to clean the water can be dangerous to mermaids if they remain too long, and the steep sides and ladders make it difficult for mermaids to climb out. Nevertheless, sometimes mermaids looking for pollution-free habitat or roomier living space have no choice but to hopscotch from pool to pool.

SHIPWRECKS
Mallows Bay Ghost Fleet, MD

Shipwrecks may seem like spooky places to call home, but many sunken ships become artificial reefs teeming with life. Algae, barnacles, mussels, and corals first colonize these wrecks, and bigger organisms like fish and mermaids soon follow. Some ships that have outlived their usefulness are actually cleaned up and sunk on purpose, or "scuttled," to create habitat on river, lake, or ocean floors.

Shipwrecks provide mermaids with valuable shelter, especially in places where there are few other natural hideaways. Mermaids make use of the mazes of decks and inner chambers, as well as the artifacts they may find inside, turning unexpected items like metal boat hooks and anemometer cups into jewelry.

Great Blue
Heron

American
Shad

120

URBAN PLUMBING MERMAIDS

Lincoln Memorial Reflecting Pool, Washington, D.C.

By now it should be obvious that mermaids, when determined enough, can show up just about anywhere there's water. While most are sensitive to pollution and limited space, some simply aren't bothered and will make a home in just about anything, from a particularly deep puddle to good-sized drainpipes to

THE BIZARRE AND BAFFLING

There is truly no end to the surprises that come with studying mermaids. Just when scientists think they understand our underwater cousins, some new adaptation is observed, be it extraordinary, dangerous, or downright weird.

Consider electric mermaids. Most mermaids have the ability to sense electrical currents via their lateral line, but some mermaids have the ability to discharge electricity, too. Just like a zap from an electric fence, this can be used to deter predators and stun prey.

Mermaid fins occasionally come equipped with venomous spines. These contain a toxin that can sting or stun a predator that might try to grab on. Despite being vertebrates, other mermaids have been known to mimic invertebrates like jellyfish, right down to poisonous tentacles that can inflict painful burns. On the other hand, some mermaids are immune to the stings of such toxic animals and actually prefer to live among their dangerous trailing tentacles as protection. Similarly, some follow in the shadow of fearsome predators like sharks, or even

122

physically attach themselves to the predators' sides, which gives them a free ride while they provide occasional services to the predator. Others have tails made up of the eight strong arms of an octopus, complete with rows of suckers.

Then there are the wonderfully strange mermaids that almost defy description. One type of mermaid mimics a flounder, a flat fish that lies on its side on the ocean floor. Because it always lies on the same side, over time its eyes migrate to one side of its head. Some deep-sea mermaids have bioluminescent lures that attract prey. Others are able to take in air or water to puff themselves up in size to frighten predators. Some tropical mermaids have pectoral fins so large they can use them as wings, leaping from the water at top speeds and gliding over the surface. If a mermaid—or you—can dream it, it seems it's possible.

What other surprising adaptations might mermaids reveal to us in the future?

MERMAIDS
AND YOU

MERMAIDS AND YOU

From tiny mountain streams to the vast ocean waves, mermaids are some of the most special creatures on the planet. They're diverse, adaptable, and surprising, and they make up only a tiny part of the amazing interconnected web of life all around us.

Mermaids play crucial roles in protecting our wild world—and so can you. By staying curious about all kinds of animals, plants, and habitats and treating all these things with care and respect, you are already well on your way toward keeping our planet safe and healthy.

Keep your eyes, ears, and imagination open—mermaids could be anywhere!

CONSERVATION NOTE

Almost all trash that doesn't get disposed of properly ends up in waterways, where it can sink or be pushed by currents into enormous floating garbage rafts. Many pollutants, like oil, float on the surface and can coat mermaids when they rise into the air. While mermaids have the means to clean themselves or avoid garbage patches, they often come across animals who are not so lucky. Sea turtles wrapped in old fishing line, whales sick from eating plastic, birds caught in pollution spills—many are rescued by mermaids. But they need our help, too, to make sure litter is picked up and pollutants never have the chance to reach our precious waterways. Other ways to help mermaids include using less water and disposable plastic, respecting wildlife and plant communities, and exploring where our water comes from and where it goes.

Many of the conservation efforts carried out by mermaids in this book, such as restoring plants and corals, protecting endangered species, and cleaning up trash are also work that people on land are doing every day. For every threatened habitat, scientists, conservationists, and concerned people like you are helping to restore and protect aquatic environments. It's very likely that your community or state has water-protection groups. Places like your state park and forestry services, department of natural resources, zoos and aquariums, or federal organizations like the National Park Service, US Forest Service, and National Fish and Wildlife Service are great places to start looking!

WHAT KIND OF

YOU'RE BUILDING YOUR DREAM HOUSE! WHERE DO YOU BUILD IT?

There's a bustling village nearby. Where do you build?

Right in town to be close to all your friends and favorite shops.

Out along the water—you enjoy peaceful scenery and the sounds of nature.

On a sandy beach

OR

In a forest glade

OR

Near something unusual, like a rock arch or ancient ruin

What kind of music do you play as you decorate your house?

Something upbeat and fast to keep your energy up.

Something soft and mellow to create a peaceful atmosphere.

You have some extra space. What do you build there?

A sanctuary for animals.

An epic jungle gym.

MERMAID ARE YOU?

Where would you prefer to hang out?
- By a swimming pool. → CORAL REEF
- In front of a roaring fireplace. → FJORD

What does your ideal bedroom look like?
- Bright, sunny, full of potted plants, and perhaps a little messy. → SARGASSUM DRIFT
- Dark, peaceful, and strung with twinkle lights. → MIDNIGHT ZONE

What's your decorating style like?
- You like swapping out decor and changing colors around. → HEADWATER STREAM
- You put up your favorite pictures and artwork that you love to look at all year. → FLATLAND RIVER

How big is your dream house?
- Three stories with lots of rooms and space! → GLACIAL LAKE
- A few small cozy rooms are perfect. → POND

What's growing in your garden?
- Lots of lush flowers, shrubs, and vines. → SWAMP
- Anything unusual, like mosses and carnivorous plants! → KETTLE BOG

What kinds of parties do you host?
- Bonfires where you play music and look at the stars. → CAVE
- Costume parties with themes, games, and prizes. → SHIPWRECK

KEEP EXPLORING!

Mermaids Near Me

Find an aquatic habitat near you, like a pond, stream, or beach. Make observations on the types of plants and animals you see, and make hypotheses about what kinds of mermaids might live there.

Me as a Mermaid

Draw what you would look like as a mermaid. Use inspiration from your favorite fish, marine mammal, or other aquatic animal—or make up something completely new!

Wild-Looking Mermaids

Look up some pictures of strange-looking fish, like flatfish, pipefish, or seahorses, and draw what they would look like as mermaids!

Mermaid Jewelry

Mermaids use items they find in nature to make jewelry. Collect some things from your yard or a nearby park and create your own accessories! (Make sure it's okay to collect things from a park before you do.)

Mermaids at Work

Look around to see if there are environmental issues, like pollution or trash, that

ACKNOWLEDGMENTS

I will be forever grateful to my agent, Valerie Noble, for leaping on this project from the outset. Another huge thank-you goes to my editor, Kate Farrell, for polishing this wild bit of speculative scientific fantasy. Thanks also to my designer, Class A Wizard Aurora Parlagreco, and Jackie Dever, Mia Moran, Mandy Veloso, and all the rest of the Henry Holt team. Thanks for all your professional deliberations about mermaid facts.

My heartfelt appreciation goes to John Morgan, who was the first editor to pick up this work. Thank you for believing in this book from day one—I hope you can still see your fingerprints on its pages. And thanks for telling me about that awesome squid.

I'm deeply grateful to so many scientists who fielded bizarre questions and provided feedback about mermaid habitats and biology. Most fundamentally, I want to thank my amazing friend, marine scientist, and mermaid enthusiast Julia Snouck-Hurgronje, who was the first and most frequent person I called to discuss the adaptations and behaviors of mermaids. Another big thank-you goes to limnologist Dean DeNicola for helping me organize and build the Still Freshwater and Wetlands sections. I am also grateful to Emily Crampe, Charlie DeVoe, Cory Tanner, Danny Caine, Kerry Foltz, Emily Knuutinen, and Justin Anderson for answering questions about different habitats. Thank you to the Armistead family, especially to Miss Lucy for being my model for the Oxbow Lake mermaid.

And then there are the people and organizations who didn't realize they were helping me, as I trawled through educational material provided by parks, conservation groups, universities, and good old fish nerds: American Fisheries Society; American Rivers; Ausable River Association; Clemson Cooperative Extension; Lake Scientist; Maui Invasive Species Committee; Narragansett Save the Bay Exploration Center; the National Audubon Society; National Geographic; the National Oceanic and Atmospheric Administration; the National Park Service; the Nature Conservancy; Ogeechee Riverkeeper; Sea Grant; the South Carolina, Georgia, and Monterey Bay aquariums; South Florida PBS; the University of Arizona Water Resources Research Center; the US Forest Service; the US Fish and Wildlife Service; and the DNRs, state park services, and fish-and-game services in nearly all fifty states.

I'm so very grateful to the teachers and staff of Pendleton Elementary School for being heroes, trailblazers, and mentors to their students.

Thank you to my parents, who first taught me that nature, science, and fantasy are all interconnected. Thanks to my dad for helping me tease out mermaid respiration, macroinvertebrate ecology, and good examples for different habitats. Sorry some of your more colorful examples from nature didn't make it in (this is a children's book, Dad). Thanks to my mom for giving me honest feedback about illustrations as only a mom can, and for all the positive ions during development. Thank you to the rest of my family for your support.

I always thank my daughters in my acknowledgments, but this is the first book where they actually had a direct role in its development. They were the first ones to read so many of these habitat passages and the first ones to see so many of these illustrations. Lucy posed for the Freezing Lakes mermaid and sketched me suggestions for different underwater scenes. Amelia helped me develop and test out the habitat quiz at the end of the book and lobbied hard for the inclusion of a flatfish mermaid. Thank you, girls—this book truly wouldn't be what it is without you.

Finally, thanks to my husband, Will, for always encouraging me on this voyage. I love you.

ABOUT THE AUTHOR

EMILY B. MARTIN grew up looking for fairies under mushrooms and giants on mountaintops. The daughter of two scientists, she learned at an early age that nature and fantasy are teammates, and that belief has shaped her dual career as a park ranger and storyteller. During the summers, she works as an educational ranger in national parks across the country, which fuels her off-season work as an author and illustrator.

To Emily, water has long been a fascination. No matter where she is, she loves tracing how animals, plants, history, and geology always flow back to water. After several years getting to know the geysers of Yellowstone, the meltwater of Glacier National Park, and the waterfalls of the Great Smoky Mountains, it wasn't a stretch to see magic in every rivulet and puddle. There was no doubt about it—mermaids are everywhere!

When not on duty in national parks, she lives in South Carolina with her husband, Will, and two daughters, Lucy and Amelia. A graduate of Clemson University with a master of science in park and protected area management, she also enjoys baking, playing music, and adventuring with her family. Her other books include the eco-fantasy Creatures of Light trilogy and the Outlaw Road duology.

Find her online at emilybmartin.net and @emilybeemartin.

The author on duty in Glacier National Park.

Emily often carries a watercolor sketchbook with her to document her adventures.

Sampling macroinvertebrates in a Great Smoky Mountain stream.

The author at an alpine stream crossing in Glacier National Park.

This work is not endorsed by the National Park Service.